tough love

She closed her eyes and sank into the darkness of the kiss, her arms gently pulling him over to her side of the car. After what seemed a long time she felt his hand under her T-shirt, on her back, his fingers under her bra strap.

She should stop him.

Instead she pushed herself further towards him, her back arched, her breasts touching his shirt, her mouth eager. After a while she found herself sliding down the seat, her knees bent up against the dashboard.

Other books by Anne Cassidy

The East End Murders series

Point

You don't grass people up

tough love

Let the police do their own dirty work

Anne Cassidy

SCHOLASTIC

Scholastic Children's Books
Commonwealth House, 1–19 New Oxford Street,
London, WC1A 1NU, UK
a division of Scholastic Ltd
London ~ New York ~ Toronto ~ Sydney ~ Auckland
Mexico City ~ New Delhi ~ Hong Kong

First published in the UK by Scholastic Ltd, 2001

Copyright © Anne Cassidy, 2001

ISBN 0 439 99811 5

PART ONE
wanting tony

1

How hard could it be to tell the truth? Gina Rogers worried about this for many hours. All she had to do was open her mouth and say the words, let the story unfold, explain the events while they were still clear in her memory.

She allowed herself a thin-lipped smile at this. As if she could forget.

That day, after the hospital visit, Gina stumbled home and went up to her bedroom without saying a word to anyone. She sat down in front of her mirror and looked at herself for a long time. Had she changed over the previous few weeks? Did she look different? She took a brush from her drawer and began to pull it roughly through her hair.

The hospital ward had been a warm place – too warm, she thought. The radiators sizzled at the touch, pumping out heat, making the room feel like a furnace. Gina had broken into a sweat and had had to push her face up to a tiny window opening on the landing. A nurse had stopped and asked her if she felt all right, if she needed to sit down. *I'm not ill*, she had wanted to say, *it's just that I'm sick to my stomach*.

Instead she had walked down the long corridor and left the messy business behind her. In the hospital room that was like a prison cell, where a policeman clung to every sign of life that came from a sick boy.

Gina knew that she would have to talk. It didn't matter that her family would be upset, that the neighbours would disapprove, that her friends would look coolly at her. No, that's not true, it did matter. But it had to be done anyway.

There'd been a visit to the police station, hours of questioning, a statement. Her dad had sat at her side, his fingers nervously tapping on her shoulder, his face waxy and drawn. Every now and again he'd turned to her and told her that everything would be all right.

Her mum had stayed at home. Gina imagined her rigid in an armchair, her feet twisted round each other, her face paralysed with incomprehension.

Kate, her best friend, had surprised her the most. She simply hadn't understood.

"Why are you doing this? You should let the police do their own dirty work. You don't grass people up. You know that!" she'd said, shrugging, looking at her out of the car window while Jonesy was revving up, impatient to get away.

When Gina had watched the car disappear up the road she'd felt as though the pavement was jelly beneath her feet. There had always been Kate. As far back as she could remember Kate had always been there at her side.

The police made the arrest almost immediately. It was in the local newspapers and it was mentioned on the regional news on television. Gina and her mum and dad had kept themselves to themselves. They each stayed in their own part of the house; her dad in the kitchen, her mum in her bedroom; Gina, a solitary figure, in the living room, using the remote to flick wildly from channel to channel.

She had been right to do it. She kept saying it over and over to herself. *I have done the right thing*.

A couple of days later she'd woken to hear her mother sobbing downstairs.

"Look at this! Look! Look at my front door!" Her voice rung through the house.

Pulling herself out of bed, Gina could hear her dad mumbling below.

"Now, now, it's not as bad as it looks. A bit of white spirit will sort it out."

Gina scrambled down the stairs and found her mum standing rigid beside the front door. Her dad was further away, leaning heavily on the end of the banister. The front door was wide open. Out in the street she could see some small kids pointing and laughing. A couple of the neighbours stood holding their pints of milk, unable to take their eyes off the scene.

The word BITCH was painted across the door in black paint. Gina gasped at the sight. It was all in capitals, which somehow made it worse. She felt herself go weak and retreated towards the stairs.

She had known that someone would find out. She had expected some payment, some grim reward for her signature on the bottom of the statement. She had realized, as she took the police car to the spot on the river, that her name would become the subject of rumour and gossip

Her mother was nodding her head as if this was what she too had expected right from the beginning. Her dad held his hand out, but it was too far away for Gina to grab. She crumpled on to the stairs and put her head in her hands. Everyone thought she'd betrayed him. But they had it wrong. She had done the right thing.

If anyone had been betrayed, it was her.

It started the week of the McDonald's fight. The time when the van came into Honey Lane with the Nike trainers. That was the beginning. When she saw Tony Campbell for the first time.

Wait, that's not strictly accurate. She'd seen Tony Campbell hundreds of times. He'd gone to the same school as her, hung around the same streets and youth clubs as she had. He'd mixed with the same kids that she'd mixed with.

No, the day that the stolen Nike trainers had come into Honey Lane was the day she really *saw* him for the first time.

The day she fell in love with him.

Their home was a small house on a council estate just outside North London, close to the M25. Half a dozen streets of bungalows, terraced housing and low-rise flats. Not that anyone called it a council estate. It was known locally as a housing development and named "Millennium Place".

It was the council's pride and joy and it housed people who had moved out of crumbling tower blocks years before. The brick dwellings stood amid small gardens and tree-lined streets. There was a large shopping centre just ten minutes' walk away and a tube station that went straight into central London.

Gina and Kate and all the other local kids still thought of it as "the estate". It was an affectionate term though, with none of the images of vandalism, broken lifts and rubbish strewn around. Gina liked living there. She and her mum and dad lived ten doors away from Kate's family. They had a small garden at the front and back. It was a friendly place and there were people there they'd known for years, since living in the high rise.

The other good thing about the estate was that it blended into the surrounding streets in many ways. The houses were built in an old-fashioned style and merged easily with others in the area. Not like the high-rise flats that sometimes seemed like they were set apart from the everyday world below. The streets around were similar, yet different at the same time; older and bigger houses, some shops and a pub, a park and a small market.

There was one big difference. The area around the estate was culturally mixed. There were lots of black and Asian families living there.

The estate was white.

Not that Gina noticed at the time. That's not true. She had noticed, but it hadn't *registered*. Just like she'd noticed Tony Campbell day after day for years.

Until the time of the McDonald's fight; the same week that the Nike trainers came into the street.

That was when everything changed for her.

2

The McDonald's fight was unexpected. The place was full of people from Gina's school. The younger kids weren't allowed out at lunchtime but they went anyway. They bought fries and burgers and relaxed in the cool air-conditioned atmosphere, while the car park outside was hot and dusty and filled with impatient vehicles edging forward in the Drive-Thru queue.

It was Gina who first noticed the line of boys from their school lounging against the perimeter wall, their school sweaters and ties discarded and hanging over the neat row of bushes that edged the parking area.

"Look who it is," she said, pointing to the far end of the car park.

Among them was a year ten boy who had a reputation for being hard. He was a short kid who had closely cropped hair and a birthmark under one eye that looked like a purple teardrop.

"Looks like trouble," Kate said.

Fights were an everyday part of school life. There were always rumblings of arguments, grudges and verbal warfare; from time to time a fight would flare up like a small electric storm that was noisy and loud and moved on in moments. And it wasn't just boys. Gina had seen a couple of ugly girl-fights that seemed to brew up over hours with all sorts of go-betweens stirring up the hurt feeling. Passing each other in a corridor, a single word or a sideways look was all it took for a slap or a punch to be thrown, a clump of hair pulled hard or a set of nails dragged across the skin.

"I'll bet there's going to be a fight!" Kate said in an excited whisper.

Fights outside school were different. They involved kids who were unknown. They were *unpredictable*.

Gina stood up holding her fries and drink, her rucksack hanging awkwardly over her arm. Kate followed, her burger in her hand, her school sweatshirt tied loosely round her waist.

Some of the boys from their school were horsing around pretending to be boxers and squaring up to each other. The boy with the purple teardrop wasn't moving. He was leaning back against the wall holding a bike chain. It was heavy and brassy to look at and he seemed to fondle it as he stood waiting for something to happen.

"There's definitely going to be trouble!" Kate said, a look of delight on her face.

A loud revving sound came from round the corner and made Gina look behind. A black van whooshed past her into the car park and screeched to a halt a few metres from the boys.

A load of other kids from Gina's school had tumbled out of the restaurant and stood watching. For a few moments nothing happened. The vehicle and its occupants sat perfectly still. Gina and Kate and the rest of the kids seemed to hold their collective breath and the only sound was the throb of music that came from deep inside the van.

Then the doors flew open and three young men got out. One of them, a boy with bleached blond hair, was holding a baseball bat.

Gina felt Kate's hand on her arm and stood watching intently.

There were a few seconds of uneasy silence as the two groups of boys eyed each other up. From behind were distant sounds from the restaurant and the queue of the Drive-Thru moving slowly forward. Gina looked from one group to the other, from one boy's face to the next. Kate's fingers were pushing into her skin and from behind she heard whispers of other school kids wondering what was happening.

Suddenly the boy with the birthmark swore loudly and swung the chain around his head. One of the boys from the van bowed low and took a run at him, knocking him back into the wall.

After that it was chaos.

The onlookers surged forward towards the fight, and Gina and Kate were carried along with them. There was shouting and squeals, and Gina stood uneasily on a low wall to see what was happening.

Two boys had another pinned up against a wall. One was pounding him with his fists and the other was kicking hard. The boy was shouting for help and had one arm covering his face and the other across his groin. Gina closed her eyes in shock and then, feeling Kate's nails digging into her skin, looked again to see the blond boy with the baseball bat aiming at the knees of another.

Afterwards, she would have sworn she'd heard the crack of the wood against bone as the injured boy folded up and collapsed on to the ground clutching at his leg. A dreadful wail came from him and the blond boy seemed momentarily startled as if he hadn't expected his blow to cause any pain. Behind him Gina could see the boy with the purple teardrop swinging his chain back and forth. He seemed to catch her eye for a moment as he did it. Then, taking aim, he swung towards the head of the blond boy who turned just at that minute. Gina closed her eyes tightly as the chain skidded across the hapless boy's face.

He let out a scream and threw the bat towards the boy with the chain. It missed him and bounced off the nearby bonnet of a car. A crimson streak appeared on his face and he touched it and looked at the blood on his fingers. The other two boys came towards their friend and pulled him backwards towards the van.

The chain was lying on the concrete and the fighting had stopped, but there were still words and threats flying about as the van revved up loudly and pulled out of the car park. In the distance there was the sound of a police siren and many of the younger kids who had been watching took flight in the direction of the High Road. Kate and Gina stood dazed, looking at the boys from their school, who were red-faced, out of breath and near to tears. On the floor, in the middle, one of them rolled about holding the back of his knee and crying unashamedly.

A police car pulled into the car park, its light flashing, two officers leaping out and walking towards the bruised group, their sweaters and ties still hanging limply on the bushes.

"Let's get out of here," Kate said, pulling Gina's arm.

But Gina didn't seem to be able to move. She

tried to swallow a couple of times but her throat was tight and a feeling of revulsion was creeping over her. It hadn't been exciting at all. It had been nasty and raw. The schoolboys who had looked so relaxed and amiable a few minutes before were now ashen-faced, sitting or kneeling by their injured friend. In a van a few miles away was a blond boy whose face had been split in half by a bike chain.

"Come on," Kate said, walking away.

Gina gave a few tight coughs, brushed her shirt down with her hands and followed her friend out of the car park and back towards school.

3

They were still talking about the McDonald's fight when the van with the Nike trainers drove into Honey Lane a couple of days later. It was a hot May afternoon and Gina and Kate were sitting on a wall going over the story again.

"Twelve stitches! Will he have a scar?" Gina said.

"Yes, but he'll be able to have plastic surgery later," Kate said, peeling the wrapping off a Mars bar as if it was a banana.

"How awful," Gina said, remembering the blond boy turning round just as the chain travelled through the air.

"And the year ten kid's knee is broken in two places. He'll be in plaster for a long time, Jonesy told me. He knows the kid's brother from the market," Kate added, knowledgeably.

Edward Jones was Kate's boyfriend. They'd been going out together for over six months. Jonesy had left school a couple of years before.

Gina sat back. The McDonald's fight was the gossip of the school. News of it had flown around until it seemed like every single student had been in that car park witnessing it. In a couple of short days it had become a kind of legend, with the boys from their school taking the status of heroes. It would be talked about for days and weeks. Eventually it would be forgotten by everyone except the two boys who bore the marks of it. They would remember it for a long time to come.

Gina watched Kate pop the last bit of her Mars bar into her mouth as a high pitched squeal sounded and a van came round the corner at speed and parked untidily about ninety metres along.

It was cream coloured, rusting at the corners. A man of about twenty-five jumped out of the driver's side and beckoned to the two girls. Gina recognized him as Mickey Campbell, who used to live a few streets away. She looked at Kate with surprise. Then Kate stood up, fluffed her hair with her fingers and walked towards him.

It was a typical thing for Kate to do. Feet first into everything. Gina knew that every school report her friend had ever had pleaded with her to *"think before she acts"*.

Gina was different and she knew it plainly enough. She thought too much before she did anything. Teachers were always saying, *"If only Gina showed more initiative."* Or, *"Gina spends too much time planning work. She needs to achieve more…*" She was the sort of person who was happy sitting in her room planning her life out in days and weeks and years. But actually doing any of it? Not likely.

She sat and watched while Kate chatted to Mickey Campbell at the side of the van. Kate was standing in a silly, girlish way, one leg tucked behind the other, her fingers pulling away at bits of her hair. Mickey's shoulders were rounded and he was looking cagily round the street. Gina thought then of his younger brother Tony, whom she knew vaguely. He'd been at her school, but had left a couple of years before and she occasionally saw him around on his way somewhere.

Mickey Campbell had been in prison once for burglary, everyone knew that. Since he'd been released he'd turned himself into a "business-man". He bought and sold stuff – a bit like Del Boy, off the telly. He was always flogging leather jackets and clock radios. Everybody, including Gina's mum, used to say that it was surplus stock or flood-damaged goods, but deep down they all knew that the stuff – some of it anyway – was nicked. It just made people feel better to pretend otherwise.

She could see Kate nodding her head in a rapid-fire way, turning and skipping back towards her.

"Quick!" she said, in a half-whisper. "Mickey's got a load of nicked trainers in the back of the van. They used to be in his lock-up, but he's had the word that the police are going to do a search. He wants somewhere to put them."

"Where?" Gina said, immediately nervous.

"Some in yours, some in mine?"

"My mum'll go mad!"

"It'll only be for an hour. His brother Tony's coming round to pick them up in a mate's car. They'll be gone by five at the latest. Your mum doesn't get in from work till late."

"But my dad's…"

She was about to say that her dad would be at home, in the garden, as he always was. But today he wasn't. She remembered that he had gone down for an appointment at the Job Centre.

Kate seemed to have made up her mind anyway and was halfway along the street to tell Mickey Campbell. Gina followed reluctantly. In a flash, the back of the van was open and they were faced with a wall of trainer boxes, fifty or more.

"Quick, you go and open your front door. Here, take these," Kate said and Gina found herself balancing five boxes of trainers.

"I really appreciate this girls, and I'll see you all right." Mickey Campbell said, his arms full of boxes.

It took about ten minutes. Gina's hallway was stacked up and so was Kate's. A couple of other people came out of their houses and watched in a kind of detached way.

"I won't forget this," Mickey Campbell said, when they'd finished.

He got back into the driver's side and a blast of music came from the radio. They stood and watched while he did a three-point turn. He was about to move off when he stopped abruptly. A police car had come silently round the corner and parked about ten metres in front of him. Gina heard the sound of a couple of front doors closing.

"Pretend you haven't seen them," Kate hissed at Gina. "Make out we're not interested."

"Mr Michael Campbell. Am I right sir?" the policeman said, standing at the driver's door of the van.

Mickey Campbell took a moment to light a cigarette before he answered.

"What of it?"

"Driver's licence please, sir?" the policeman asked, unperturbed by Mickey's answer. Gina noticed that his eyes scanned the houses behind the van. The other policeman had got out of the car and was looking around. Gina caught his eye for a second, then she looked hurriedly away.

It was Sergeant Hamley, the policeman who

had come into their school a couple of times to give talks. She remembered him, standing at the front of the class, giving a quick smile and writing his name in chalk on the blackboard.

"Hamley," he'd said, in a friendly voice, "like the toy shop. Only don't think you can play around with me."

It had got a few laughs, but the officer had gone on to show that he wasn't just a comedian. Some of the tougher boys had tried giving a bit of lip, but he had put them in their places with some stinging words. Gina wondered whether Kate had recognized him.

"Here."

Mickey Campbell gave over his licence and, without looking at it, the first policeman passed it across to Sergeant Hamley.

"Do you have any objection to us looking in the back of your van, sir?"

Gina linked her arm in Kate's and they stood rigidly a few metres away. A mumbled answer from Mickey Campbell made Gina stiffen more. He handed the keys to the officer and sat moodily back in the seat. She knew that there was nothing in the van, but still her breath caught in her chest as she waited for the sergeant to walk the six or seven steps round the back and open the doors.

She looked at Mickey Campbell sitting in the

driver's seat, staring straight ahead. At the sound of the doors closing she saw his eyes crease up at the corners. He was smiling to himself. Sergeant Hamley walked back up to the front of the van and handed the keys back.

"I'm sorry to have troubled you, sir."

Then he took his hat off and ran his fingers through his hair in a weary manner.

"Let's go, Frank," his partner said.

Sergeant Hamley put his hat back on before turning to Gina and Kate and looking at them for what seemed like a long time. Kate managed to keep a pleasant smile on her face but Gina had a mouth full of saliva and was swallowing rapidly.

He knew. *The sergeant knew it all*. Gina was sure.

"Drive safely, sir," he said, his words still smooth. "Goodbye girls," he smiled at them. "We'll meet again some time, I shouldn't wonder."

And then he was in the car and gone. Gina felt a lead weight in her chest that had come from nowhere. Sergeant Hamley had seen through the whole thing, and would now be looking out for them.

Mickey Campbell was grinning widely.

"I won't forget this, girls. Tony'll be round in an hour to pick up the goods!"

He gave them a wave as he drove out of the street.

"I feel awful!" Gina said, looking at her watch, wondering how long it would take for the next hour to pass. A lot more than sixty minutes, she was sure.

"What's the problem?" Kate said, getting some gum out and sliding it into her mouth.

"We've just broken the law, that's what!" Gina said. "What if that policeman comes back? He could find out where we live! He could ask us for information!"

"We didn't see anything. We didn't hear anything. That's all."

"It's not right. Not really," Gina said, weakly. A few minutes before she'd been concerned about the boys in the McDonald's fight. Now she had something new to worry about.

"Oh, come on. It's only a few pairs of trainers. It's not like you're robbing someone or anything. They get their money back on insurance."

Perhaps Kate was right. It wasn't like they were actually hurting anybody. Any individual *person*.

"And anyway, we might get a pair of trainers out of it!" Kate said, her shoulders hunching with anticipation.

A new pair of trainers. That was how it all started.

4

Tony Campbell was nineteen, with jet-black hair that had a streak of grey at the front. Just one streak, as though someone had touched it with a paintbrush. Gina looked at it for a long time as he picked up the boxes of trainers, three at a time, and carried them out to the blue car that was waiting outside.

She hadn't noticed it when he was at school. He seemed like a completely different person from the red-faced kid she remembered. He'd got much taller, she was sure, and his shoulders looked wider. He seemed to fill up the narrow hallway and she had to stand back against the wall as he passed, only centimetres from her.

"Still at school, Gina?" he said, balancing boxes in his arms.

"Yes." She nodded her head for longer than she needed to, her voice hiding down in her throat somewhere.

He took the last few boxes along the hallway. All the time Kate was at the front door looking up and down the street to see if anyone was coming. A few minutes later all the trainers were safely out of the house and in the boot of his car.

"There's something different about you, Gina," Tony Campbell said, standing on the pavement, his eyes scanning the street. "You've got bigger or smaller or something."

He was looking her up and down, his eyes sweeping across her chest and down to her shorts before lazily looking back up again.

He kept using her name, *Gina*, as though he specifically remembered her from school. It gave her a light-headed feeling and she held his gaze for only a moment before looking down and wiping some imaginary crumbs from her top. Kate gave her a playful shove and stood close to Tony Campbell, adopting a little girl expression.

"I expect me and Gina deserve a reward for helping you and your brother out."

Tony Campbell's eyes crinkled up and he patted Kate on the head.

"I expect you do," he said, opening the car boot. "What size feet have you got?"

"Size seven for me and Gina takes a four," Kate said, moving her shoulders up and down with exhilaration.

Tony Campbell passed a box of trainers backwards to Kate, who jumped up and down on the spot before running off to her own house. Pulling another box out he turned to face Gina.

"Such small feet," he said, lowering his voice and looking straight at Gina, "such *baby* feet."

She could have swooned right there and then. Instead, she looked intently at a passing car until it turned out of the street. Coughing lightly into the back of her hand she caught his eye again and found herself smiling stupidly. He took her arm lightly and led her to a nearby garden wall and she sat heavily on to the dusty bricks.

"Luckily, I have some baby trainers," he said in a gravelly voice, and squatted down in front of her with the shoes.

He took one of her sandals off and held her foot in his hands for a moment. She looked away, embarrassed. What was he doing? What did he want?

"Prince Charming, me," he said, his hair shining in the late-afternoon sun.

A couple of kids nearby had stopped playing and were looking at them. Somewhere in the far edge of her vision she thought that Kate had come out of her house again.

Tony Campbell slid the stiff trainer over her foot.

"I can do it up myself," she said, her voice quivering.

"I'm sure you can," he said and with his fingers he traced a line up her leg until it got to the edge of her shorts. She looked at his hand on her skin and wanted to clasp it, to hold it tightly. She glanced up and met his eyes, his face only centimetres away from hers.

"You've grown up a lot, Miss Gina. I shall have to keep an eye on you," he whispered, pulling his hand away.

"Do they fit, Gina?" Kate's voice broke in.

She dragged her eyes away and saw her friend walking and dancing up and down in bright white trainers. Tony Campbell stood up in front of her and looked up and down the street and then at his watch.

"I'm just putting them on," she said, clearing her throat, the skin on her leg tingling.

"I have to go. I'll see you well-dressed young ladies around."

Tony Campbell got into the driver's seat of his car as Gina was still threading the laces through the tiny holes of the shoes. In a moment the engine roared and the car was gone, leaving the heat of its exhaust hanging in the afternoon air.

5

Her mum was furious, but it wasn't about the trainers.

Gina was downstairs in the living room. Her dad was in the kitchen getting the evening meal ready. Gina could smell garlic and onions and meat. She felt pleasantly aware that she was hungry. The TV was on but she wasn't really watching it. She kept holding her feet out, one by one, inspecting her new shoes and thinking about the afternoon.

Her mum came in just after six. She walked straight into the living room and sat down heavily in one of the chairs. She still had her jacket on and her shoulder bag flopped on to the floor. Her work badge was still on the lapel of her jacket and Gina read it over, even though she knew what it said: *Harts Building Society: Ms Donna Rogers*.

"Hi," Gina said, smiling at her mum, tucking her feet into the base of the chair.

"Where's your dad?" her mum said dully, pulling her sandals off.

There was no need to answer because her

mum could hear him in the kitchen. Just then he shouted, "Is that you, Donna?"

"Course it's me. Who else would it be?" her mum said under her breath.

"Dad's been cooking something special," Gina said, lightly.

"Has he been to the Job Centre?"

"I'm sure he has. He's been out all afternoon," Gina said.

She was telling the truth. Her dad hadn't come back until after five. He'd been carrying two plastic bags full of vegetables that looked like they'd come from the market. The Job Centre was nearby, Gina knew.

Her mum leaned back in the chair and stretched her arms above her head. Gina could see the long painted nails that matched her lipstick.

"But did he get a job?" she said tersely.

The door opened and her dad's head appeared. In his hand he had a spatula.

"Hello love, tea's ready soon."

"Did you go?" her mum said.

"I popped in. Like I said I would."

Her dad's voice had dropped. Gina knew what it meant. He had gone into the Job Centre but there hadn't been any work for him. At least not the kind of work that he wanted.

"Did you ask them for a job?" Her mum's eyebrows had dipped to a point in the middle.

28

Gina wondered why she was asking when it was obvious that her dad didn't have a new job. She braced herself for his reply and felt relieved when the living-room door swung shut and her dad retreated to the kitchen. Her mum tutted loudly, stood up and went out of the room. Moments later Gina heard her footsteps up the stairs and then the sound of a door slamming.

Gina felt herself sink further into the sofa. Now there would be a long silence where her parents would politely avoid each other. She would probably eat her tea with her dad while her mum feigned a headache or lack of hunger and stayed upstairs.

It hadn't always been like this.

After being made redundant from the car showroom Gina's dad had spent some months looking for another job. Sales were down though; cars from abroad were cheaper; all over the country men were packing up their belongings and closing their desk drawers for the last time.

"You'll get another job," her mum had said at first.

Her dad had bought the local and national newspapers, sent off applications, rung around all the contacts he had had in the motor business. None of it led to a job.

Her mum had continued to be supportive.

"Lots of people go through a period of un-employment," she'd said, brightly. "At least I'm working. We can still pay the bills."

One day, Gina had come home from school with Kate and found her dad in the living room shoving bits of paper into a black plastic bag.

"What are you doing?" she'd said.

"Thirty-three companies I've applied to and not got one interview. Not one! I've had enough."

"Oh Dad, don't be silly."

"Anyway. I don't want to work in a car show-room any more. I wasn't any bloody good at it – that's why they *let me go*. I've had enough of trying for jobs that I can't do and nobody wants me for."

"Good for you!" Kate said. "My Jonesy is like that. He doesn't want to work for anyone, he says. That's why he's got his own stall down the market. He's his own boss."

Gina's dad looked at Kate for a few moments and then his face broke into a thin smile.

"That's it, Kate. Perhaps I should try and be my own boss."

When Gina's mum came in from work that day she looked at the black plastic bag full of application forms, trade papers and Job Centre advice and seethed. She sat down in the armchair and spent a long time painting her nails flame red, shaking her hands in the air and blowing on each individual nail. Then, flexing her fingers as though doing some kind of exercise, she walked into the garden where Gina's dad was working. Gina, a feeling of foreboding settling on her, turned the TV off and went upstairs to have a shower.

When she'd finished she stood in the fog of steam and heard the voices from downstairs. Her dad was speaking loudly, even shouting at times, but every few moments her mother's voice sliced through his words until the front door slammed and finally there was quiet. A little later, when she'd finished getting dressed, she walked out on to the landing to find her dad sitting on the top stair, his head in his hands.

It was the first time she'd seen him crying. But it wasn't the last.

Now there were no rows. Just angry silences and closed doors. Now and then her mum might sound off at her dad, telling him how useless he was and how he'd let her down, but her dad wouldn't respond. He'd just immerse himself in cooking or gardening or looking under the car bonnet.

She couldn't face a meal sitting alone with her dad, each of them listening for sounds from upstairs. She had no appetite for it now. She left the TV on and slipped out of the front door, making sure that it closed quietly behind her.

A few streets away from Honey Lane there was a small precinct of half a dozen shops; among them an off-licence, a launderette and a fish and chip shop. It was a focal area for kids to hang around and Gina usually saw people she knew there. Outside the chip shop were a number of teenagers leaning against the wall hanging on to white paper cones of chips and cans of drink. The smell of frying food was overwhelming and she remembered her hunger. Passing by a boy from her street she dipped her fingers into his bag and fished out a couple of steaming chips. Ignoring his protests she looked around and saw two black girls that she knew talking outside the off-licence. One of them was Eve Cole, a girl from her class in school.

"Hi," Gina said. "Have you seen Kate?"

"Saw her in Jonesy's car about half an hour ago," Eve said.

"Oh," Gina said, dismayed.

Kate and Jonesy out in the car. It usually meant that they were out for the evening. Eve's friend, a small girl with tightly-beaded hair nudged her and whispered something.

"She getting engaged to him?" Eve said.

"Dunno. Maybe. I'm not sure," Gina said, uneasily.

Kate was always boasting about her future with Jonesy.

"What about her exams?" Eve said, as though Gina had just answered yes to her question.

"You know what she's like," Gina said, dismissively.

"I like the trainers," Eve said.

Gina held her foot up in the air. She liked them too.

"Remember when we all bought the exact same trainers?"

Gina smiled. She did remember. She, Kate and Eve had all gone shopping on the same day with their mothers and had all come back with the same make and colour of shoes. Gina hadn't even expected to buy shoes and Kate only got hers because her dad had won some money on the races.

Years ago, when they'd just started secondary school, the three of them had been friends. They'd sat in the same bunch of desks and had their packed lunches at the same time. They'd hung around in the playground and walked home from school together

Since then they had drifted apart. Eve had started to hang around with some other girls, and Gina and Kate had kept themselves to themselves. There hadn't been a row or falling-out, but it just seemed that Eve was always in the company of another crowd. Gina still chatted to Eve from time to time because she usually knew everything that was going on before anyone else.

"How's Marvin?" Gina asked.

Marvin was Eve's younger brother by a year. They had often had to drag him round with them because Eve had been told to look after him.

"He's all right. He thinks he's boss but…"

Just then a car came round the corner and pulled up to the kerb. An electric window opened smoothly and Tony Campbell leaned out.

"Hi Gina, fancy a drive?"

Gina looked around with embarrassment and caught Eve's curious expression. She shrugged her shoulders.

"I'm waiting for Kate," she said, nervously brushing the front of her T-shirt.

"She's out with Jonesy. I saw them a while ago. I'm just going up to the Track. I'll only be a couple of hours, then I'll drop you home."

"I don't know," she said. She hadn't told her mum or dad.

"Come on. I'll be back at nine tops."

He was smiling at her, looking her up and down again. She stood rooted to the ground with indecision. He glanced at his watch for a second. If she didn't say something he would drive off and she would lose the chance. She made up her mind.

"See you later, Eve," she said, striding towards the car. "If you see Kate, tell her where I've gone."

As she got in Tony Campbell started the car and drove off up the street without a word.

6

The Track was a disused sports centre. Years before it had been the venue for amateur athletics meetings and school sports days. There was a six-lane running track and alongside it a ramshackle wooden stadium. All the local schools had used it once. Gina's school had had to use coaches to reach it. There were a couple of old brick changing rooms with communal showers and toilets. Gina remembered that they were usually inhabited by families of harassed-looking spiders and the odd mouse that appeared and caused mayhem for a few moments.

The local council closed it down some years before and it had been gradually taken over by the young. During the day, local kids used it as a base for playing football or riding BMX bikes around the track. At night it was often used by older kids, some who came in cars and on bikes. There were stories of parties and drugs and sex in cars, but nobody really knew the truth of what went on. It wasn't a place that girls went to without accompanying boys. Gina hadn't been there since she was eleven, when she used to ride her mountain bike awkwardly around the chalky track.

"How are the trainers?" Tony Campbell asked.

"Fine," she said, stiffly.

She shouldn't have come. She felt funny and hadn't been able to think of a thing to say since she got into the car. That afternoon she'd been thrilled by Tony Campbell's attention; now she felt out of place. The Track was only a mile or so away and they'd soon be there. All sorts of vague worries began to swirl about in her chest. Why had he asked her to go up to the Track? Did he think she was the sort of girl who would have sex with him? Did he expect her to? Her stomach seemed to take a dip and she looked round, out of the back window, to see familiar streets disappearing in the distance.

She definitely shouldn't have come. Tony Campbell was nineteen. He hung around with his brother and older blokes who spent their time in pubs and clubs. Gina knew for a fact that he'd had an older girlfriend for over a year and there'd been talk of him getting engaged. He was in a different league to her and her friends. He'd been nice to her that afternoon, he'd flirted with her, made her feel special. But he was older. He would have expectations. For all she knew his asking her to come up to the

Track was a code that she hadn't known about. Was it the same as saying *will you have sex with me?*

"What's the matter?" Tony Campbell said, glancing back over his shoulder.

"Nothing," she replied, her voice shaking a little.

"Here we are," he said, his car slowing down.

Gina looked out and saw the sign that said: COUNCIL PROPERTY – ENTRANCE FORBIDDEN. The car turned into the narrow lane that led up to the old sports centre.

It was still light and there were some young kids coming away, walking their bikes down the uneven dirt track. Tony Campbell had put his lights on and was moving slowly forward.

"I've just got to see a couple of mates," he said, giving her a smile.

She nodded. He had arranged to meet someone there. Maybe it wasn't going to be so bad.

"You're allowed to speak," he said.

"I know," she squeaked and then cleared her throat with two small coughs.

They turned into the old coach park and Tony Campbell pulled the car up beside a parked jeep. A couple of young men and a striking blonde girl were lounging against it. One of the men had his head tipped back and was drinking from a can of lager. Gina recognized the girl. It was Shelly Martin, whose dad owned the off-licence on the precinct. She'd gone to Gina's school, but had left a couple of years previously.

"Come and meet the Thompsons," Tony Campbell said.

Gina was glad to see that there was a football game in progress and a number of other kids around, some that she recognized from school. She got out of the car, her anxiety easing. He took her arm immediately and pulled her in the direction of the jeep.

"These boys are seriously well off," he said quietly to her. "See that jeep? It was a birthday present from their old man."

One of the young men turned towards them. "All right Tony?"

He was tall and thin, wearing a light linen jacket and pale-coloured trousers. Underneath the jacket was a shirt and tie. He looked like he was about to go for a job interview. Glancing past him, Gina could see that his brother was dressed in a similarly formal way. Shelly Martin had a dress on, long, and flowing almost to her ankles. It looked like it was too expensive to be worn in the middle of a disused athletics track.

Tony Campbell was the same. He had trousers and an open-necked shirt on. On his feet were brown leather shoes. No trainers, no jeans, nothing casual. She looked down with dismay at her own clothes. Her T-shirt was too tight across her breasts; her shorts showed too much leg. If she had known she would have dressed up. She had nice clothes but they usually stayed under plastic covers in her wardrobe while she spent most of her free time in jeans.

Stopping a couple of metres in front of them the young man's attention turned immediately to Gina. Her hand rose up and she found herself fiddling with the neck of her T-shirt. The other brother smiled, but stayed talking in a tight knot with Shelly Martin. Tony Campbell spoke.

"Paul, how goes it? Did you see Chalky? I left the gear round at his place."

"Picked it up about an hour ago. Good stuff. It'll go well."

Paul Thompson looked quizzically at Gina.

"This your little sister?"

"Leave off. Gina's a mate. She helped me and Mickey out this afternoon."

Gina found herself suddenly disappointed. Tony Campbell considered her a *mate*. That was all. She felt her legs go limp under her.

"A bit young, but nice-looking," Paul Thompson said, looking mildly interested.

"Watch it. She's with me," Tony Campbell said, putting one of his arms around her shoulders and playfully pulling her towards him.

She perked up, straightening her back. For a brief moment she caught Shelly Martin's eye. She gave a half-smile, but the other girl didn't seem to notice and went on talking.

"I thought Luke had packed Shelly in," said Tony.

"You know what they're like. One minute it's on, the next it's not," Paul Thompson said, fishing a wallet out of his back pocket. "How much did we say?"

"Two hundred."

"I thought it was a hundred and fifty?" Paul Thompson pulled a wad of notes out.

"Please, Paul. Don't mess me around."

Paul Thompson put his hand up in mid-air.

"Only a joke," he said as he pulled out four pink notes and handed them over.

Tony Campbell held each one up to the fading light, as if he were checking its authenticity.

"Come on. They're real. Straight from the Bank of England."

"Only a joke."

Gina smiled, as if amused. Inside she was trying to keep calm. Tony Campbell was being paid for the stolen trainers. It was highly illegal. The words *receiving stolen goods* came into her head and she looked down guiltily at her own new trainers. Sergeant Hamley's face came into her head. *If he could see her now.*

"See you at the weekend?" Paul Thompson was walking away.

"Yes. In the Spider?"

Gina watched Paul Thompson nod his head and walk back to his brother. The Spider's Web was a pub by the river that was popular. Gina had passed it once or twice and wondered when exactly she would have the confidence to go in.

"Come on, you look like you're cold." Tony Campbell was folding each of the pink notes up individually and sliding them into a leather wallet.

Once in the warmth of the car she realized that she had felt chilled. She rubbed her arms as the driver's door clicked shut. Tony Campbell turned to her.

"Don't forget your seat belt," he said and leaned over to pull the belt across her.

She heard the click and found herself looking straight at him, his face only centimetres away. Without a word he kissed her on the mouth.

It lasted only seconds, as if he were tasting something to see if he liked it, she thought. He pulled away and looked at her. His fingers came up to her face and traced a line that went down her neck, on to her chest. She could feel the line still tingling as his hand rested lightly on her breast.

He kissed her again and she opened her mouth and let her tongue reach out. For a few seconds she felt her head swimming, her neck weak, as he rubbed his fingers back and forth across her nipple.

She took his hand and moved it away, kissing him more fiercely as she did it. After a couple of moments he stopped.

"I'm sorry," she said, apologizing.

"It doesn't matter," he whispered and she saw his face break into a smile that she couldn't read. "OK, Miss Gina. Let's get you home."

He turned the ignition and they drove carefully off, avoiding the kids playing in the semi-dark.

On the way back she began to talk. She told him about the fight at McDonald's and how the boy from her school might never be able to play football again. She described her mum and dad's row and her dad's lack of a job. He listened and told her about his mum and dad's new car and their holiday in Florida. His voice was light and cheerful and his fingers kept tapping on the steering wheel as if he had some tune in his head.

All the while, as she was talking, she was thinking of the kiss and his fingers on her skin. From time to time, as they drove past familiar shops and streets, she closed her eyes and tried to imagine the moment again.

It was no good though. The thrill was somewhere back in time, it had flown past and
couldn't be caught again.

7

Gina Rogers thought a lot about sex.

No, wait. That wasn't strictly true. What she really thought about was love. Not the romantic kind – the flowers, heart-shaped balloons and Mr Right. Rather she found herself looking for something more down to earth – a flesh and blood person like Kate had found with Edward Jones.

She'd begun to have these thoughts at the beginning of her final year at school. She'd sat through hot September days when the sun forced its way between the broken window blinds and the chalk dust hung like mist in the classroom. She'd looked hungrily out of the window for something new, some other kind of life. She'd imagined someone leaning against the school railings waiting for her to come out; not a boy, but a man. The thought had thrilled her. A young man who smelled of work and pubs and cars, not just bubblegum and sweat. Someone who had closed the door on adolescence and stepped out into the grown-up world.

Someone like Jonesy.

Sex was part of it. She'd included it in her wish list.

She'd imagined a partly-lit bedroom with soft music coming from a CD-player. On a bedside chair were her clothes, folded, except for her underwear which had been thrown carelessly on top. Her head was flat on a pillow, her hair dishevelled, the sheets crumpled messily around her.

There was a shadowy figure there with her. She found herself coughing nervously when she thought of him. He was the one who waited outside the school gates. She could never quite see his face, but his skin was warm as she rubbed her hand up and down his back. She could picture, almost *feel* his mouth on her neck, his hands reaching for her below the bedclothes.

It was always the same person leaning above her, his hair falling across his eyes, his shoulders tensed and full of desire. It was like a film that ran over and over until she was dizzy with frustration.

When Kate and Jonesy had started to see each other she was sceptical. It all happened so *suddenly*. One day she and Kate were buying pop magazines and Toblerones and the next Kate was looking moody and troubled, her eyes swivelling around the playground before coming to rest on knots of sweaty boys. They'd still been friends with Eve Cole then and Gina had found herself paired off while Kate flirted with the boys, their older brothers and the young male schoolteachers.

"You'll get yourself into trouble," Gina had hissed.

But Kate, coming back from the bushes behind the gym, just laughed. Her skin was crimson from close contact and she had bright red lovebites on her neck, which she pretended to try and cover up. All afternoon she would feed them with the details, a spoonful at a time until the whole experience lay on a plate before them. Gina's best friend, who found school and learning so unpalatable, had found something she liked the taste of – the opposite sex.

Edward Jones worked on his uncle's clothes stall in the market. He was nineteen but looked older. He was bright and nice and Kate knew him vaguely through some friend of her dad. One day when they were strolling past the stalls there was a notice up that said, PART-TIME STAFF WANTED. Kate had nudged Gina excitedly.

"Here's a chance to make some cash!"

Gina watched from a few metres away as Kate fluffed her fingers through her hair and waited patiently for Edward Jones to finish serving a customer. All the while she was wondering whether her mum and dad would let *her* work in the market. Would she have time to do her schoolwork? She'd already written to Sainsbury's though. What if she got a part-time job on the stall and then they wrote to her offering her a job filling shelves?

Kate was standing, looking up at Edward Jones, talking rapidly. Gina couldn't hear what she was saying, but she went on for ages. She was about to take a couple of steps forward, to introduce herself, but Kate turned suddenly and walked back towards her, hooking her arm and pulling her off up the road.

"He's told me to come on Saturday morning. He's going to try me out!"

"Does he need anyone else?" Gina said.

"I dunno. You could ask him," Kate said, excitedly. "We could work together!"

She meant to go back the next afternoon after school. Instead she gave Sainsbury's a phone call. No, they didn't have any vacancies at that precise time. Yes, her name was on the waiting list. No, she needn't ring again, they would contact her if they needed her.

When she returned to the market it was too late. An older man told her that the other job had been given to someone else just that afternoon. She'd missed it. It was the story of her life; she'd hesitated, thought too much about something. She'd gone home feeling a sense of loss, as though she'd let something important slip by.

Kate and Jonesy got together quickly after that. It was love, Kate had said after only a few weeks. On Kate's sixteenth birthday, Jonesy bought her a ring. Kate said it was an engagement ring. Gina could hardly believe it.

"You're only sixteen!" she said, incredulously.

"We're not getting married, for goodness' sake! At least, not till I leave school. Jonesy wants me to do all my exams and go to college."

Jonesy this and Jonesy that. Even though Gina got tired of hearing Edward Jones's opinions on everything from global warming to the price of chips she couldn't help but like him.

"Come with us, Gina," he often said when picking Kate up in his car.

And with Kate's persuasion she often did. The pair of them didn't seem to mind her coming along. Her presence didn't bother them. They included her in lots of things; cinema outings, McDonald's, drives out in the country, shopping. They simply didn't mind.

Gina enjoyed it. She liked Jonesy's sense of humour and Kate's affection. She didn't even mind it when the pair of them merged into a kiss that seemed to last for hours. She watched while Kate's hands disappeared up inside Jonesy's shirt and he cried, jokingly, *Stop! Stop! Help me, Gina. I'm being molested!*

She liked Jonesy a lot. Too much, she sometimes thought. Not that she had any intention of easing him away from Kate. None at all. It was just that he became a kind of blueprint for the person she wanted.

Just after Christmas she found them in bed together.

She'd gone into Kate's house just as Kate's parents had been going out.

"She's upstairs with Jonesy," Kate's mother had shouted, leaving the front door ajar for her.

She'd just left the stony atmosphere of her own house and was feeling low. She'd gone up the stairs, grumbling to herself, wondering whether she could persuade Kate and Jonesy to go to the cinema with her. She'd thrown the door open expecting to see Jonesy lounging on the bed and Kate curled up at his feet.

Instead they were both in the bed, joined together in a deep kiss, their naked shoulders above the duvet. Part of her wanted to walk straight out again, but instead she stood rigidly at the door looking at her friends as though they were complete strangers. It took a few seconds for them to register the open door, to notice Gina standing there, her mouth slightly agape, a look of shock on her face.

Kate saw her first and buried her head into Jonesy's chest in a snort of laughter. Jonesy looked round and his eye met with Gina's. At first he had a look of concern on his face, almost a look of shame. But with Kate in a spasm of giggles beneath him his expression broke and his look seemed to say, *I'm sorry Gina, you're not meant to see this*.

Embarrassment flooded through her and she turned and walked away, letting the door close behind her. She took the stairs two at a time and went out of the house as though someone was chasing her. She kept walking along the street, round the corner, a few streets further and along by the shopping precinct. She saw some of her other mates and went and stood with them. After a while, Eve Cole walked past with her brother Marvin and she stood and chatted.

Inside her was a mixture of shame and outrage. How could she have walked in on them like that? What would they think of her? How long had they been having sex? Should she have known? Wasn't Kate afraid of getting pregnant?

When she saw Kate the next day she asked her outright.

"I won't get pregnant!" Kate said cockily.

"Everyone says that."

"But I won't, because I'm taking these."

In Kate's hand was a small silver packet of pills.

"I take one every day for three weeks. Then I stop and have a period. This way I definitely won't get caught."

"What if your mum finds out?" Gina picked up the packet of pills and looked closely. Each pill was in its own bubble and beside it was a day of the week.

"My mum knows. She's the one who took me to the doctor! Look, Gina, they know how serious me and Jonesy are about each other. One day before Christmas my mum said to me, *If you're having sex with him, you need to make sure that you're protected*. At that time we hadn't actually gone the whole way, but I told Jonesy and he thought it was a good idea."

"And your mum lets you have sex in your bedroom?"

"Not exactly. She doesn't actually say we can. It's a sort of unspoken thing. We make the most of the times they go out…"

Kate had a grin on her face and Gina had to smile.

From then on Gina looked at Jonesy in a different way. She became a little shy of him and didn't go out with them so often. She hung around with some of the other girls and spent the odd hour chatting to Eve Cole.

When she was on her own though, she couldn't help but think of the two of them, Kate and Jonesy lying together tangled up in a duvet. She longed for that sort of relationship. All she needed was the right person. A grown-up; someone she could trust, who would look after her.

Someone like Tony Campbell.

8

It hadn't exactly been an arrangement, but Tony
Campbell picked Gina up outside the off-
licence three days later. *I might be able to see
you on Thursday. I'll take a chance and drive by
the precinct about sevenish. I can't promise
though.*

Gina had run home from school, dumped her
books in her room, showered and dressed and
found that she still had almost two hours to kill.

Her dad had been curious.

"What are you in such a hurry for?"

"I'm popping out," she said.

The question had thrown her. There was no
reason why she shouldn't have said, *I'm meeting
someone*. But she wasn't really. He had only said
he *might* be around. If she told her dad where
she was going, it would be like admitting that
she was really expecting him to be there. And
if he didn't turn up her disappointment would
be huge.

"You'd better take your key. I might be out
later," her dad said.

"With Mum?" Gina said.

"No, your mum's got her night class. I thought I might go out for a pint."

"That's a good idea," Gina said.

Her dad needed to get out of the house. He was depressed and spent too much time on his own. It didn't help that her mum was always carping at him for not having a job. She felt this rush of emotion for him and gave him a quick hug.

"You smell nice," he said. "Isn't that your mum's perfume?"

"I borrowed some. She won't mind."

At half-six she left the house. Glancing along the street she saw Jonesy's car parked outside Kate's. She took a step towards it, but then stopped. It would kill some time if she had a quick chat with Kate and Jonesy. On the other hand, she had no idea whether they were alone in the house or not. She'd be embarrassed if she rang the bell and interrupted them. So she took a slow walk in the direction of the shopping precinct.

Turning the corner by the off-licence she saw Eve Cole's brother, Marvin, and a couple of his mates, talking to a policeman. It was Sergeant Hamley. His expression was stern and his voice low and hard. Marvin was standing looking bored, his eyes gazing past the policeman. The other boys were anxiously paying attention.

Gina couldn't hear what was being said and

she sidled past the group and went into the off-licence. It had only been a couple of days since the officer had spoken to her and Kate, saying, *We'll meet again, I shouldn't wonder*. She looked down at her feet and saw the white trainers staring guiltily back at her. She watched as Marvin Cole and his friends walked off, and saw Sergeant Hamley look around the precinct and rest his eye on the window where she was standing. For a moment their eyes met and she found herself coughing gently, the back of her hand covering her mouth.

The policeman gave her a quick smile and then walked off in the opposite direction. Gina felt light-headed with relief. Then she laughed at the stupidity of it. What had she got to fear? So, she'd been given a pair of trainers by a friend. How was she supposed to know that they'd been stolen? Honestly.

She picked up a packet of chewing gum and paid for it. It wasn't as if they could prove her trainers were actually *stolen* anyway. Who was to say she hadn't bought them in a shop? In the back of her head she heard the beep of a car horn. Grabbing her change, she walked briskly up to the shop door. Once outside she slowed down and looked at Tony Campbell's car. She gave a half-surprised smile, as though she'd just remembered their arrangement.

"I thought you'd forgotten," Tony Campbell said, when she got in.

"I was just getting some chewing gum."

He leaned over and kissed her lightly on the mouth. Just a second, no more. She hadn't been expecting it, hadn't even had time to close her eyes. Then he was putting the car in gear and accelerating off up the street, while she was struggling gleefully with her seat belt.

He took her to the Spider's Web. He bought some drinks and carried them out to the garden where she was sitting. He was talking about his job.

"Most of the time I work in that hi-fi show-room on the trading estate. Paul Thompson works there as well."

Gina knew where he meant. A giant ware-house store just off the dual carriageway. She remembered Paul Thompson from the visit to the Track. She pictured the wad of notes he had had in his hand, and the way he and his brother were dressed.

"I thought you said they were rich?"

"They are. Their dad likes them to work though. He just buys them a lot of stuff. And they make a bit extra from other things. Like me. Now and then I help my brother out."

"Like the other day?" Gina said, thinking back to the van-load of trainers.

"Not always like that. On my mother's life, it's mostly legit stuff. A bit of driving, delivering, that sort of thing."

"Doesn't your brother worry about getting caught?"

The words came out too quickly and Gina immediately wished she hadn't said them.

"Why should he get caught?" Tony Campbell said, his forehead creasing up.

"No reason. I just wondered whether he ever thought about it."

"Nah. Anyway, it's all small fry stuff with him. A few knock-off jeans, trainers, leather jackets. The police have got bigger stuff to worry about: murderers, rapists, bank robbers. That's who they should be looking for."

"How come Sergeant Hamley wanted to search his van?"

Tony Campbell laughed out loud.

"Hamley put him in prison years ago for burglary. Every now and then he likes to check up on him. He thinks he's a hard man. It don't bother Mickey. He thinks it's funny."

Would he have laughed if the policeman had found the trainers in the back of his van? Gina thought it, but said nothing.

"Don't you worry about my Mickey. He can look after himself. We can all look after ourselves, come to that. Now, Miss Gina. What about another drink?"

She gulped down her drink more quickly than she'd have liked to. Then she handed her glass to him. He took a twenty-pound note from his wallet and walked towards the pub door. He had trousers on, not jeans. His shirt sleeves were folded up to his elbow. The streak of grey in the front of his hair made him look older than nineteen. He looked like a young businessman. It gave her pleasure to see him like that. His jacket was hanging around the back of his seat. She felt the fabric and saw the label inside. The make was famous; it had probably cost a lot of money. She looked around the pub garden with some pride. This man, in these smart and grown-up clothes, was with her.

She'd had a boyfriend before. After Kate had got serious with Jonesy she'd gone to a party and ended up dancing with the cousin of a girl from her class. His name was Martin Wilson and he'd held her so tightly that she'd thought she might not be able to breathe. After a few slow dances he'd asked her if she wanted some fresh air.

In the dark of the garden they'd stood up against the climbing ivy and he'd kissed her over and over. She hadn't really had a good look at him but she joined in enthusiastically, opening her mouth wide and letting her tongue slide about.

After a while he'd slipped his hand under her top and she'd backed away shaking her head. He hadn't seemed to mind and she'd relaxed again, enjoying the kisses. But every few minutes he tried again, his hand coming from different angles, and she had to keep breaking off the kissing to stop him. In the end she felt worn out.

"Pack it in, will you?" she'd said finally.

"It's all right," Martin had replied. "I respect you for not letting me."

It had been some kind of test. He had wanted to touch her and yet if she had let him he wouldn't have respected her. What kind of logic was that?

She'd gone out with him a couple of times only to find his hands wandering all over her. As soon as they were on their own, in the park, in the cinema, in her kitchen, he would lunge at her, his hands sliding over her clothes as though they were covered in oil. When she stopped him he kept saying *sorry, sorry*. It was as if he wasn't really in control of them. When she finally got fed up and pushed him away he would hold his hands in mid-air as though she were pointing a gun at him.

"I really respect you," he said. "I won't force you."

She stopped seeing him. His need for her made her feel ill. She didn't like him much anyway. The only thing he talked about was West Ham football club, and his brother's new car.

The sun was setting as Tony Campbell walked back out into the garden with the drinks. It was like an orange ball glowing on the roofs of the houses that stretched down towards the west. The pub garden looked dark in comparison. Tony Campbell put the drinks on the table. He positioned his chair in front of hers and sat with his legs apart so that her legs fitted in-between. His face was close to hers and she thought for a moment that he was going to kiss her again in front of everyone in the garden. He didn't though. His fingers touched her hair and after a while he started to tell her about his last girlfriend.

"Michelle was twenty-one. Worked in a travel agent's. I met her at a club. She was different to you, taller and blondish hair. Everyone thought we were going to get engaged."

He let go of Gina's hair and sat up in his seat. His legs were tightly packed against hers.

"She had different ideas, though. She was doing this night class thing and then suddenly she decided she wanted to go to university. One minute she was a working girl and the next she'd had enough. Wanted to go back into education."

Back to school. All Gina wanted was to get away from it.

"Is that why you broke up?"

"Partly."

He picked up his glass and drank some of his drink.

"What about you?"

"Me?"

He wanted to know about her past. Her boyfriends, her experience.

"Oh, I've had ... I've had a relationship."

It wasn't a lie. The word *relationship* made it sound more than it was.

He smiled at her. It was a knowing smile, as if he saw right through her claims.

"Gina, it's what I like about you. The fact that you haven't been around."

He leaned forward again, a hand on each thigh, his mouth close to her ear.

"Why don't you drink up and we can go for a drive?" he whispered, his mouth brushing against her ear lobe.

Her hand was shaking as she picked up her glass and drank it down.

They parked in a lane that was adjacent to the river. She was in a state of frozen excitement and hadn't been able to make conversation. She heard him turn the engine off and pull up the handbrake. Further along the lane were other parked cars, nestling against bushes and trees, mostly hidden in the shadows.

The car was silent and she turned to see him

taking his seat belt off and brushing his trousers down with his hand. Then he leaned back in his seat with one arm leaning casually against the steering wheel.

"What do you think of the view? A real Lover's Lane."

Martin Wilson would have been all over her by then. She would have felt his rushed breath in her ears and his grasping fingers, and inside her there would have been a growing revulsion.

Tony Campbell reached over and turned the radio on. The back of his hand brushed her knee and she tensed. The tinkling sound of a piano came on as he turned back to her, put his hand on her neck and started to kiss her slowly, his mouth only half-open, his finger drawing circles under her ears.

She closed her eyes and sank into the darkness of the kiss, her arms gently pulling him over to her side of the car. After what seemed a long time she felt his hand under her T-shirt, on her back, his fingers under her bra strap.

She should stop him.

Instead she pushed herself further towards him, her back arched, her breasts touching his shirt, her mouth eager. After a while she found herself sliding down the seat, her knees bent up against the dashboard.

When his hand was on her thigh she felt a

ripple of pleasure that made her legs ache. Her hands reached around his back, rubbing hard at his ribs. Without rushing, his fingers found the hem of her skirt and pushed it up.

A sound from outside made them both stop. A car had screeched to a halt behind them and a door slammed angrily. There were raised voices and Gina sat up abruptly, pulling her skirt and T-shirt down. Someone had seen them. They had gone too far. It wasn't allowed. Her shoulders slumped down with guilt.

"Look at that," Tony Campbell said, his voice bemused. "It's Luke and Shelly."

She turned and looked out of the window. The jeep was parked at an angle. Shelly Martin was marching away from it, and Luke Thompson was rushing after her. After a few seconds she stopped, and he stood by her, trying to put his arm round her shoulder. It was too dark to see very much and they were too far away to hear the words. The body language was clear. Shelly Martin was angry about something and Luke Thompson was trying to make it up.

"Lovers' tiff," Tony Campbell said. "They're always rowing, those two."

Then he used his fingers to turn Gina's face away from the window and back towards him. When she was facing him his hand dropped and rested on her breast.

"I…" she started to say.

"Shh…" he whispered, kissing her neck.

But it was no good. Her mind was on the couple out in the lane. Her shoulders and arms felt rigid. The moment had gone. She was too aware of herself. Even the music on the radio was different, fast and jarring.

"I'm sorry. I…"

Tony Campbell sat back and rubbed her shoulder.

"Nothing to be sorry for. I'll take you home."

He wasn't angry, he didn't even seem to be upset. He put the car into gear and started to do a three-point turn. Gina could see the outline of Luke and Shelly in the headlights of the car. They were still talking heatedly. Tony Campbell touched his horn lightly and the couple looked round like startled birds. When they recognized the car they both waved. Neither of them looked happy.

As they drove off, she heard Tony Campbell tutting and saw that he was shaking his head. He gave her a quick smile though and after a while began to sing along with a song on the radio.

It was all right. She began to feel good again. They'd talked. They'd kissed. He'd touched her but it hadn't gone too far. She'd called a halt to it and he hadn't minded at all.

"You all right?" he said, turning the music louder and accelerating away from the river.

"Fine," she said, reaching across and squeezing his arm.

9

The back of Jonesy's car was like an oven. Gina and Kate were sitting with the windows and the sun roof open, trying to draw cool air inside. They were both still wearing their school shirts and trousers; their ties and jumpers lay crumpled on the seat. Between them was a giant bag of crisps and two empty cans of drink. The car was parked alongside a cash and carry warehouse on the industrial estate, and Jonesy was inside picking up some stock for the next day.

"Let me get this right," Kate said, lifting her feet up and resting them across Gina's knees, "Tony Campbell took you to the Spider's Web, plied you with drinks then drove you to the river for a snog."

"No, not exactly."

Trust Kate to sum it up so ungraciously.

"I hate that word *snog*. It sounds so messy, so undignified."

"That's because it sometimes is. What did you do? In the car, I mean?"

"We just kissed..."

"Come on, Gina. Tony Campbell's nineteen. He was virtually living with his last girlfriend. You telling me that he took you to the pub, bought you drinks and didn't expect anything in return?"

"Not everyone's like that!"

"Most blokes are."

"He told me he likes the fact that I'm not … experienced."

"That's just a line, Gina. If it's true, how come his last girlfriend was older and had been around?"

"Maybe he likes the fact that I'm different!" she said indignantly. "And anyway. Most blokes aren't like that. Jonesy wasn't!"

Kate was about to speak and then stopped. She grinned mischievously, picked up her school tie and wrapped it round and round her hand.

"You're right. Jonesy was different. It was me that jumped on him."

Neither of them spoke for a minute. The only sound was the crinkling of the crisp bag and an occasional crunch. Kate had told Gina over and over about the trouble she had getting Jonesy to go out with her.

He said he was too old for me! Every Saturday when I turned up for work I used to ask him to go for a drink or a coffee. I even invited him round my house when my mum and dad were out.

"You're a kid!" he said. "I can't go out with a kid." Eventually, I went down the cash and carry with him and when we were loading up the van I kind of accidentally fell against him. I don't really know how it happened but we started kissing. After that, he couldn't make any excuses. I just wouldn't take no for an answer.

Gina had believed every word. Kate had taken one look and decided she wanted Edward Jones for herself.

"How long have you and Jonesy been together?" Gina said.

"Let me see," Kate said, looking as though she was doing a complicated sum in her head, "seven months, one week and two days."

Gina sighed. She hadn't been with Tony Campbell for even a week.

"Anyway," Kate's voice was suddenly serious, "that Tony Campbell. Don't get too involved with him. You don't really know much about him."

"Why do you say that? What have you heard?"

Kate usually knew loads of stuff. She got it all from Jonesy who was a mine of information. He seemed to know just about everything that was going on in the local area; the pubs, the clubs, the offices and even, because of Kate, the schools.

"All I know is that Jonesy was upset when I showed him my new trainers. He said something about the Campbells being involved with these rich kids and getting in too deep."

"The Thompson brothers?" Gina said, remembering the notes that Paul Thompson had taken out of his wallet.

"Drive a jeep? All suited up?" Kate said.

Gina nodded.

"That's them. They live in this detached house near the river. Their dad's not a nice character, bit of a crook. Did a bit of time for GBH – grievous bodily harm – Jonesy said."

"That's nothing to do with Tony though."

"No, but apparently he's always out with them. That's all. It might mean he likes that sort of stuff."

Gina's lips puckered and she didn't speak. Kate wasn't telling her much that she didn't already know. Tony Campbell himself said that he did a few jobs for his brother. And it wasn't his fault if his friend's dad was violent.

Just then they saw Jonesy coming out of the warehouse laden down with an armful of dresses and trousers. He was shouting something as well. Gina guessed he wanted them to come and help him but Kate just rolled the window up, put her hand to her ear and kept saying, *What? What? Can't hear you.*

When Jonesy got to the car, she rolled it down again.

"What were you saying?" she laughed.

"I said I wanted my assistant buyer to come and help."

"Shall I come?" Gina said, lifting each of Kate's legs off her own.

"Creep," Kate said, laughing.

Gina smiled at each of them. Really, when it came down to it, she loved spending time with Kate and Jonesy. Up to then there had been *almost* nothing she liked doing better.

10

Tony Campbell's parents were much older than Gina's. They were both in their sixties and looked more like grandparents.

"This is my mum, Shirley, and my dad, Ronnie," Tony Campbell said.

"Hello, Gina," his mum said, smiling.

She was wearing a matching top and trousers, emerald green velour with a swirl of sequins sewn across one shoulder. Her hair was beige and heavily lacquered into place. His dad's hair was almost gone and what was left was white. He was wearing a sporty tracksuit and smelled strongly of aftershave.

"Your mum works in the building society, doesn't she?" Shirley Campbell said.

"Yes."

"I've seen her there. Very smart lady. Very polite too."

Gina smiled with pleasure.

"Will you have some tea or coffee, maybe?"

"Good idea," Tony Campbell said. "I've just got to make a couple of phone calls. Then we can go up to my room and listen to some music."

Gina followed Shirley and Ronnie into the kitchen. Between them they made the tea. She filled the kettle, he got the tea bags out. She found the mugs and he placed the milk and sugar on the table. Finally, one of them produced a large tin of biscuits. On the front of it was a colour photograph of a black and white kitten.

Ronnie Campbell was humming as he was pouring milk into the mugs. Gina looked past him to the window sill behind the sink. Along it were several china teapots all with cat motifs. One of them was actually shaped like a cat, a paw acting as the spout and the tail curled up to make a handle. Another was just a giant cat's face with the spout coming out of an ear. A couple more had paintings of cats playing. They were all unusual.

Shirley Campbell saw Gina looking at them.

"Beautiful, aren't they? They're just ornaments. Mickey and Tony buy them for me. For birthdays and Christmas and occasionally because they feel like it."

"When they're trying to get round you, you mean," Ronnie said.

"He's right. Usually when they've done something they shouldn't. You know what boys are like."

"They're not boys, they're grown men!"

Shirley Campbell smiled at her husband as she poured from a stainless steel teapot. Gina didn't know what to say, what kind of conversation to make. She turned and looked at the kitchen door wondering when Tony would be back from his phone calls.

"It's nice to see our Tony with a girlfriend," Ronnie Campbell said, handing Gina a mug of steaming tea. Shirley offered her the tin of biscuits but she shook her head.

"And someone a lot better than the last little madam."

"Good Lord, yes," Ronnie said, rolling his eyes.

Gina sat up, interested. The last girlfriend. That was something she'd like to know more about.

"I think Tony thought a lot of her," she said, hoping to sound neutral. It didn't do to join in with the criticism.

"I'll say," Ronnie said.

"It was all give, give, give. My Tony adored that girl. And look how she treated him."

"We told him. She's too old for you. Too full of herself. Very opinionated, she was."

Gina looked from one to the other. Their conversation flowed as though they were taking turns.

"He was upset, I can't deny it," Shirley said,

74

dipping a biscuit into her tea. "But she had such a mind of her own. I said to him, you should get someone different. Someone who's willing to listen to other people for a change."

They both looked at Gina and smiled. She felt uneasy at their scrutiny. Did they mean a girlfriend like her? Was she the sort of person they wanted for their Tony?

"And young Luke. He's lost his girlfriend too. I don't know what young girls want these days, I really don't." Mr Campbell said it with a look of puzzlement on his face.

Just then the door opened and Tony Campbell came in.

"Come on, let's go up," he said.

Gina stood up, clutching her mug of tea. As she turned to go she noticed that Shirley and Ronnie Campbell were holding hands on the table. Their fingers were cradled together and they were both looking fondly at their son. It gave her a warm feeling. They'd been together for years and were almost old-age pensioners, but they were still in love. Behind them sat the porcelain cats, evidence of their sons' thoughtfulness and care.

It was a happy house. Gina could almost feel the contentment purring gently in the background.

Tony Campbell's bedroom looked like someone had just cleaned and tidied it. It was full of wooden furniture, like the rest of the house. The curtains and quilt cover matched and there was all sorts of electrical equipment slotted on to neat wooden shelves that were down one side of the room.

"I tidy it up myself!" he said, when she commented on it. "No one comes in here. It's private. Not all blokes are slobs."

"Sorry," she said jokingly, her hands in the air.

He wasn't listening any more though. He'd clicked a switch on his CD player and music was humming through the room. Then he took his jacket off and hung it on a hanger and put it into the wardrobe, smoothing down the other clothes that were hanging there.

"Where's your brother?" she said.

"At work? I'm not sure. Why don't you sit down?" he said, pointing to the bed.

She sank on to the duvet and leaned back against the wall. She crossed her legs and brushed imaginary crumbs from her jeans. Then she pushed her fingers through her hair, pushing it back from her face.

"Have Shelly and Luke had another fight?"

"Why do you ask?"

"Your mum was saying something…"

"Shelly's given Luke the elbow."

"Oh."

"If you ask me, he's better off without her.

She was always running hot and cold. O₁
she wanted him, the next she didn't."

"Is he upset?"

"Just a tiny bit," he said, and gave her a half-smile.

For some perverse reason this news made Gina feel pleased with herself. That relationship was over but hers had only just begun. Here she was, in Tony Campbell's house; in his bedroom. She was the right kind of girlfriend who had just chatted with his parents. They were at ease with each other; they hadn't had a cross word. She slipped her shoes off and lifted her feet on to the bed. She made herself more comfortable and sat and just watched him.

He was humming along to music, taking his wallet and credit card holder and mobile phone out of his pocket. He laid them on top of a chest of drawers, taking a moment to straighten each item. Then he walked over and sat beside her on the bed. He leaned forward and began to unlace his shoes. Sliding each one off, he placed it neatly by his bedside table.

"I like your mum and dad," she said.

"They're great," he said, sitting back on the bed and sliding his arm around her shoulder.

"I wish my mum and dad got on as well."

"Um," he said, burying his face into her neck.

"If only my dad could get a job…" she said,

closing her eyes and feeling his lips on her neck, his fingers trailing up and down her arm.

Her mind went blank. It was just as she imagined it would be. Alone in a bedroom with someone who cared about her; just like Kate and Jonesy. She wanted this.

"I like you a lot." The words just came out. She couldn't have stopped them if she tried.

"Ssh…" he whispered and lifted his finger on to her lips as though she were a tiny girl in school.

She kissed him then, her arms reaching up for him, holding on firmly while her muscles slowly turned to liquid. All the while she moved towards him on the bed, the tips of her breasts hardening and her mouth open as though she was feeding from him.

After a while he began to unbutton her blouse.

"Wait…" she said.

But he just kept kissing her and after a few moments her shirt was hanging loosely on her shoulders and her bra was undone and up around her neck.

"Wait…" she whispered, her arm covering her breasts. "What about your parents?"

Tony Campbell sat up. His hair was tousled and he looked mildly amused. He got up off the bed, straightened his trousers and walked across to lock the bedroom door.

"They won't come in," he said, smiling and holding the key in mid-air.

He sat down again and began to unbutton his shirt. He did it in a lazy way, almost as though she wasn't there and he was getting ready for bed.

A twinge of panic made her sit up. He was getting undressed. In a few minutes he would be naked; he would turn and look at her. He would expect her to have sex with him then and there on that bed. She swallowed back a mouthful of saliva.

Wasn't it what she had wanted? A real grown-up boyfriend, like Jonesy?

His shirt unbuttoned, he pulled it off and hung it round the back of a nearby chair. What was she to do? Lie back and hope for the best? Her fingers gripped tightly on to the edges of her shirt and she pulled her legs up until they were under her. She sat as still as she could; like a statue.

Then he sat back on the bed and looked at her stricken face.

"What's the matter?" he said gently, his hand rubbing up and down the skin of her neck. "Don't you care about me?"

"Yes, I do," she said, bursting with emotion, a lump of frustration in her throat.

"What's wrong?" he said.

"I'm sorry," she said, fiddling with the buttons of her blouse. Her bra was still undone beneath it, but it didn't matter. She just wanted to cover herself up.

Tony Campbell lay back on the pillow, his hands behind his head.

"You haven't done this before, have you?"

"Not much, no. Actually, not at all." She gave a few coughs.

"It's OK. It's not like a test. It's just a natural thing."

"I know…" she said.

"It's one of the reasons I like you so much, Gina. I'm sick of girls who've been around. I go out with you because you're so…"

"Young?" she said, looking warily at him.

"No … I don't know … innocent? Inexperienced? I don't know. I just like you."

She gave him a sceptical look.

"On my mother's life!"

He was telling the truth, she was sure. She let her shoulders relax and leaned back against him.

"Every time I kiss you, you get into a panic. What do you think? That I'm going to force you?"

"No!"

"If you don't want to, it doesn't matter."

"But I do want to…"

"Then that's OK too. I'll look after you. I know it's your first time. "

"But I haven't … I mean I'm not taking any pills or anything," she said thinking of Kate and the slim, silver packets.

"You don't have to worry about that. There are always condoms. They're safe."

"I don't know…" she said, feeling a flush of embarrassment at the very word. *Condom*.

She remembered them from school sex education lessons. Thin, balloon-like pouches; colourless, greasy to touch, elastic; they had rolled them on to test tubes, all desperately avoiding looking at each other or any of the lads in the class. In her mind they were rude, silly things and they had no part of her vision of love-making. After the lesson, a couple of the boys took some and filled them up to use as water bombs in the playground.

"You don't have to make a decision. It's not part of the deal. If you don't want to, then that's fine by me. You take your time, Miss Gina. When you want to, you tell me."

He gave her a hug and kissed her on the forehead. Then he got up and put his shirt back on. He changed the CD and went across to his wardrobe and pulled a tie out. He held it against his shirt for a moment. Then he began to put it on.

She was reminded of her dad. Every morning, when he had had a job, he would stand in front of his mirror and put his tie on. He had a whole bunch of them hanging from a special rail in the wardrobe. She and her mum used to laugh at him making his choice. When he walked out of the front door, he always grasped at the knot to make sure it was straight. Then he looked businesslike; as if he had purpose and importance.

She hadn't seen him in a tie for a long time.

"Come round on Saturday. My mum and dad are going to a wedding. We can get a video and some beers." Tony Campbell said. "Forget about all that other stuff. It's not important."

She looked at him standing in his shirt and tie. His jacket was hanging over his arm. He could have been anything; a young banker or a lawyer. She had a powerful longing for him and she wanted at that moment to walk over and undo the tie and put her hands inside his shirt and feel his skin against her face.

"That sex stuff. It doesn't matter to me," he said.

But at that moment it had become important to her. He was going to be the one. He was her Jonesy, and Saturday was the night that it would happen.

11

The precinct was dark when he dropped her off. She watched his car drive away until the red lights were tiny pinpricks in the distance. He was meeting the Thompson brothers for a late drink. They were going to try and cheer up Luke. She wondered where they were going. The Spider's Web? Or another pub that she didn't know about? Maybe they were meeting down at the Track.

Voices from behind made her look round.

Marvin Cole and a couple of his mates were kicking a ball. It wasn't exactly a game of football, they were just passing it to each other and larking around. When he saw Gina, he bounced the ball on his head a few times and shouted out at the top of his voice, "All right Gina! Look at me! Michael Owen!" Some of the people from the shops were looking out of their windows and Gina shook her head in an adult, grown-up kind of way.

Marvin had always been loud. When she and Kate had hung around with Eve Cole, Marvin had always been a difficult part of the equation.

Whenever they went to call for Eve he was always there, and they often had to take him out with them. He always wanted things, even though he knew that none of them had any money. *Can I have one of them? Can I? Go on, get us one? Please. I'll pay you back.* He was in tow like a small, yappy dog that they had to take for a walk.

He was in the year below them and even though he went to the same school Gina and Kate largely ignored him; even Eve, his sister, ignored him if she could. He was a big boy for his age and was always in some sort of trouble. He was never quite in uniform and his rucksack always looked as though it had been dragged down a motorway and then tossed on a rubbish dump.

He hardly ever did any school work so he was always in the bottom set, and was often sent to the year heads during lessons for misbehaviour. He always seemed to have money though. He had at least one paper round and also delivered free newspapers for his mum. Apart from Eve, he had three older married sisters and they were always giving him handouts. He was the baby of the family and Eve had always complained that he'd been spoilt silly.

When they stopped hanging round with Eve, they would see her and her new mates talking agitatedly to Marvin. Marvin was usually laughing or cheeking them back. Frequently he was holding some notes in the air or showing off his mobile phone or examining his cash card.

Marvin Cole. You couldn't walk past him in the street without noticing him. The ball rolled past her foot and she heard his footsteps behind her.

"Gina. Why don't you let me take you out somewhere nice?"

Marvin picked up the ball with his foot and raised it off the ground. He had his arms out in mid-air, balancing like someone on a tight rope.

"Please, Marvin. I don't go out with kids," she said, disdainfully.

It was all a joke though. She knew it and so did Marvin Cole. Even though he was a pain she couldn't help but laugh at his big ways. He was only fourteen but he wore the right clothes, had the best trainers and he was usually full of unlikely stories.

Marvin's mate kicked the ball back harder than he meant to and it bounced loudly off a BMW that was parked nearby. In a flash one of the shop doors opened and an older man came out.

"Clear off, you!" he shouted, looking at the roof of his car.

Marvin should have said sorry. That would

have been the sensible thing to do. But years of practice on teachers had left him more than ready for a row.

"All right, pal?" he said. "No need to wet your pants. We're only having a game."

The man, who had been about to walk back in the shop, turned around and looked aghast at Marvin. Gina put her hand on Marvin's arm and tried to direct him away. It was too late though. The man, who was probably about fifty, walked angrily in their direction. All the while, he avoided looking at them, his eyes wandering around the precinct as if he really wasn't very interested in what he was doing. When he got close enough he stopped, looked directly at Marvin, and spoke in a low voice.

"Look, you flash black bastard, you keep your mouth shut if you know what's good for you. We don't want the likes of you round here."

"Who do you think you are?" Marvin interrupted.

"Hang on," Gina said, weakly.

"You think you own this place, you lot." The man's face was taut with annoyance, his mouth barely open enough to let the words out.

"Push off, old man..." Marvin continued, but his words had a tremor in them and Gina could feel his arm tensing.

"Black filth, you are. You just dirty everything.

You can't stand to see other people doing well."

"Just a minute," Gina's voice was louder this time.

"Why don't you people go back to where you came from?"

Gina gasped. It was one thing telling Marvin off for being an idiot. It was quite another giving a load of racist abuse.

"Why don't you keep your nasty opinions to yourself," she said, louder than she'd intended.

"What's it to you?" the man said, looking hard at her. "He your boyfriend or something?"

"It's none of your business," she said, and was about to tell the man what she thought of him when she heard a sound like someone choking.

Looking round she saw that Marvin's mate had collapsed in laughter and Marvin was starting to see the funny side.

"She's your girlfriend!" Marvin's friend said, pointing at Gina.

The man was looking at each of them with a show of extreme patience. Marvin and his friend seemed to have forgotten him. They were slumped together on a low wall laughing and pointing at Gina.

"Huh!" the man said, loudly.

Gina looked weakly from one to the other. Now Marvin had spoilt the moment. The man deserved a good mouthful for spouting off the racist stuff. She would have done it as well (and even better if Kate had been with her). Now though, with Marvin on a different planet, there wasn't much she could say.

"Like I said, they should go back to where they came from."

"Why don't you go back to where you came from!" she said, turning her back on Marvin and his silly friend.

The man's eyes met Gina's and she held them for a few moments. Then he turned and walked away, rattling his car keys loudly and disappearing into the shop. When the door swung to a close she turned and walked across to Marvin and his friend. In the back of her mind she thought about telling them off. They'd put her in a difficult position and not backed her up.

"Hey Gina," Marvin said, laughing, "why don't you go back to where you came from?"

"No, man," his mate said, nudging him so hard that he almost fell off the wall, "you're the one. You have to go back to where you came from. See. Back to Africa."

"Not me, man," Marvin said, getting his mobile phone out, "I came from Barnet, me. You go back to where you come from."

"Enfield. That's where I came from. Maybe I should go back there."

"What do you think, Gina?"

There was no answer for any of it. It was all typical Marvin silliness. She tutted loudly and walked briskly away. Thank God, she thought, turning the corner into her own street, thank God that she'd left those young silly boys behind. Now she was like Kate. She had a grown-up boyfriend who had a car and a wardrobe full of smart clothes.

That made her a grown-up too.

12

When her mum threw a china mug at her dad it hit him hard on the shoulder and then fell to the floor with a crash. The dregs of coffee that were in it splashed on his T-shirt and up on to his cheek. He put his hand there as though he'd been mortally hurt. His eyes were wide open and there was a look of disbelief on his face. Gina gasped, her eyes resting on the pieces of china that lay under her dad's chair.

It was Saturday and they were having a late breakfast. Gina's toast was still under the grill and she was mid-way through pouring out some orange juice.

Her mum stood by the table, the hand that threw the mug still in mid-air, her face rigid with fury. Then, without a word, she turned and walked out of the room. When the door clicked shut there was a moment's silence, then Gina heard a deep, muffled sob from the hallway.

"I ought to go after her," her dad said, getting up.

Gina's eyes narrowed. Why should he go out

after her? It was her mum who had started the row and caused the injury.

"She's upset, you see," he said, explaining. "I upset her last night."

It's no excuse, Gina wanted to say. You're not to blame. She's the one who's being so difficult.

"I'll just make sure she's OK," he said, apologetically.

Gina looked at her dad with his wet cheek and his stained T-shirt. His shoulders were rounded with worry and his chest had sunk away to nothing. She wanted to shake him. She wanted to tell him to pull himself together. Instead, she knelt down and began to clear up the broken china.

There'd been a running row since the previous evening, when her mum had come in at a quarter to twelve from an evening out with her workmates.

Gina had been in bed when she'd heard the front door close and the sound of her dad's voice low and insistent, his words joined up. Her mum's answers had been brief and loud like exclamation marks. There'd been some walking up and down the hallway and the sound of doors opening and shutting. She'd heard a few "*ssh*"s, mostly in her mum's voice, followed by her dad's mumblings as he followed her round the downstairs part of the house. Eventually, she heard the sound of footsteps on the stairs and her parents' bedroom door open and close. She knew it was her mother because of the lightness of her step and the breathy sounds she made.

She lay on her bed with the duvet thrown aside. Her room was dark apart from a thin strip of light that came from a street lamp outside. After a few minutes she heard her dad plod up the stairs, his breathing heavy, as though he was pulling a huge weight behind him. The spare-room door opened and shut and she heard him moving around for a few minutes.

Then there was silence.

She pulled the duvet around her and lay curled up. For a long time she seemed to stare into the darkness, her mind blank. After a while she went to sleep.

In the morning the row rumbled on, her dad's face like a closed book, her mum looking sharply at him across the table, reading his expression for any sign of criticism. She'd carried on making her breakfast, avoiding looking at either, her eye resting on the window sill above the sink where Tony Campbell's parents had a line of cat teapots. In the back of her head she registered a few sulky words and then, without warning, like a flash of lightning, her mum's mug sailed through the air.

Later, when her dad had gone out into the

hall, she took care picking up the jagged pieces of china from the floor. She tried to ignore the sound of his voice; the words were unclear but the pleading tone was obvious.

What had happened to them? What about their love for each other?

Had it simply disappeared because her dad's company no longer wanted him? Had he become redundant as a husband? Maybe there had always been problems, and as a small child she simply hadn't noticed. Now that she was growing up they no longer worried if she was a regular witness to their fights.

Later, when she closed the front door behind her, she forced them out of her thoughts. That night she was due to go to Tony Campbell's. His parents would be out. She ought to be feeling good, not worrying about them. They had had their time for love and they had messed it up. Now it was her turn.

She had made plans to take precautions. All she had to do was go into a chemist and walk up to the front of the shop. There was always a stand next to the cash register. It usually held an array of packets, all different types. Gina had no idea why there were so many varieties. The teachers in school hadn't explained that. All she had to do was reach out and pick one up. As simple as that. As if selecting a type of chewing gum. *I'll have one of these*, she had to say, as bold as brass, to the shop assistant.

Buying a condom. It wasn't illegal, she knew that. She was over sixteen.

No one was to know though. That's why she was walking to the chemist on the far side of the shopping centre. That's why she had her rucksack with her so that she could bury the packet in the bottom where no one would find it.

She hadn't even told Kate. That was something she wanted to do afterwards, when it would be too late for her friend to persuade her it was a bad idea. *You've only known him a week*, she could hear Kate saying. *He hangs around with a bad crowd*. She might even advise her to tell her mum. *I confided in my mum and it all worked out for the best!*

Outside the chemist she stood still for a moment. How could she confide in her mum about anything? Her mum was so full of anger at her dad that she didn't have any room for Gina's concerns. She remembered her mum talking to her dad when she'd left. Her neat hair and pretty face, her matching red lips and nails. Would she make up with him or simply say, *I want a divorce, I've had enough*?

The thought made her legs feel heavy and her head ache. She saw her mum on her own in some flat or house, her neat building society uniform hung up inside a wardrobe, her vases and ornaments scattered around an unfamiliar room.

How could she confide in her mum?

She pushed the chemist's door open and went purposefully inside.

13

Tony Campbell picked her up in his car. She watched from the upstairs bedroom as he parked at exactly eight o'clock and walked to her front door. He was formally dressed, as though he'd just come straight from work, or some important meeting or event. He had a dark suit on and a light-coloured shirt and his tie flapped in the evening breeze. She felt a tickle of anticipation as she watched him lock the car door, straighten his trousers and pat his jacket down. He took his mobile phone out of his top pocket and fiddled with one of the keys. Then he replaced it.

He was calling to take her out. He was picking her up for the evening. Even though they were only staying in his house he had come at a certain time, as though he was taking her to some important function. Eight o'clock on the dot; as though the precise time mattered.

As the door-bell chimed she took a last look in the mirror.

Why her?

He could have had any number of girls; older

girls with jobs and bank accounts and easy, confident ways. His interest in her was a mystery. It was like an expensive gift that she had unexpectedly received.

She had her smartest skirt and blouse on. Not too dressy, not too casual. Hidden away, underneath, she had her newest underwear; lemon satin with lace trim. Her face was pale with just a touch of make-up. Her hair had been washed and meticulously blown dry so that it looked twice its usual volume. She had simple gold earrings on and a gold chain around her neck. Over her shoulder was a tiny brown suede bag that someone had bought her but that she rarely used. In it was a comb, some perfume and the packet of condoms.

From downstairs she heard voices.

"Hello, I'm Donna, Gina's mum. You must be Tony."

"Hi. Good to meet you. This is a really nice house."

"It's only eight years old. We've always been very happy here."

Gina was standing on the top landing listening. After a few moments she realized that she was holding her breath. She put the palm of her hand across her ribcage and made herself breathe slowly in and out. Her mum had her business voice on, light and friendly. Tony was being extra polite and sounded like a prospective buyer. When her breathing was normal she brushed her skirt down and checked that the buttons on her blouse were done up.

"Hi," she called, and forced herself to walk down the stairs.

"You look nice," Tony Campbell said, looking up at her.

She gave him a half-smile, her feet feeling one stair after another, her hands holding her skirt down as though she was afraid that a gale force wind might suddenly blow it up.

"What film are you going to see?" her mum said.

"Oh, some action thriller," Gina said quickly, to cover Tony Campbell's look of puzzlement.

It was true in a way. They were going to see a film. They were just going to see it in Tony's house when his parents were out.

"OK. Don't forget. Your dad wants you in by eleven."

Her mum said it with a perfectly straight face. Gina pursed her lips. Her dad hadn't said any such thing. Her dad wasn't even there. Her mum was just saying it to give the impression that her dad was in charge of things. She felt a flash of annoyance. Her dad in control, the head of the family; nothing was further from the truth.

"No problem," Tony Campbell said firmly, his hand pulling open the front door. "Nice to meet you, Mrs Rogers."

"Please call me Donna."

Gina could feel her mum's scrutiny as she walked towards the car. She turned to wave and her mum gave her an approving smile. She was pleased. Her daughter had brought her first real boyfriend home and he had turned out to be respectable and nice. Once in the car, Tony Campbell gave a pretend sigh of relief.

"Your mum looks very young," he said.

"She's only thirty-four. She had me when I was eighteen."

"Young," he said, thoughtfully. "Still, there's nothing wrong with settling down young. If you meet the right person, what's the point in waiting?"

She couldn't speak for a minute. Her voice had turned to liquid in her throat. Was he referring to her? Was she the *right person*?

"Which film shall we get?" he said lightly, the car pulling away from the pavement.

"I don't mind. You choose," she said, coughing nervously.

It didn't matter what he chose. It didn't matter what he said or what he did. Just then she knew that she would love all of it. Everything.

* * *

After the film was over he cleared away the end of a pizza and tidied up the empty cans. She plumped up the cushions on the settee. Her bag had fallen on to the floor and she picked it up and sat it on the armchair. She could hear the water running from the kitchen and the clink of the plates as he washed them up. She sat down again, crossing her legs neatly. The room was tidy and she smoothed her skirt and looked at her watch. It had just gone ten o'clock. She only had an hour left. Her eye strayed to her bag on the chair, light brown suede, not much bigger than a purse really. Inside it was the packet of condoms.

All through the film Tony Campbell had been affectionate to her. He'd put his arm round her and kissed her lightly on the mouth now and then. He'd squeezed her ribs and rubbed her arm.

He hadn't tried to touch her any more than that. Even though she curled herself up close to him and ached to feel his fingers on her skin. Her forehead wrinkled with dismay as she heard him opening and closing the fridge door in the kitchen.

She had put him off. Her previous nervousness had made him hold back. They hadn't been like lovers at all, more like good friends. He was giving her time, not making any demands. It was up to her to make the move. She would have to be explicit. He had said he wouldn't push her and now she had to show him that she wanted it to go further. If she didn't do it soon it would be too late.

"Why don't we go upstairs?" she said, when he came back in with two cans of drink.

"What's wrong with here?" he said, picking up the TV remote.

"It's more comfortable up there," she said, pulling the brown suede bag towards her.

"It's warmer down here," he said, clicking the remote.

The TV channels raced past her eyes. It wasn't as easy as she thought it would be. Didn't he understand that she was using a code? Giving him a signal? She opened her bag and fiddled about for her comb. She could feel the cellophane on the small cardboard box of condoms. Like a tiny packet of sweets they sat waiting to be opened.

"I bought these."

She blurted the words out, the packet in the palm of her hand.

"What?" he said, just glancing round and then back to the TV screen.

"I thought we could … that we might use them."

She held the palm of her hand out so that it was in his line of vision. He looked at them and turned round.

"When did you get them?" he said, looking at her strangely.

"This morning. You said we could use them. To be safe… So that I don't get—"

The words were falling out of her mouth as he took the packet from her hand and pulled her towards him.

"You didn't have to buy these."

He started to kiss her neck and then her hair.

"I'll look after you. I said I would," he murmured, his arms holding her so tightly that she could barely draw a breath. After a few seconds he picked up the remote and the TV went dead. Then he pulled her up off the settee and walked up the stairs to his bedroom.

PART TWO
loving tony

14

When life was perfect Gina worried. That was the sort of person she was. Good times, when they came, unsettled her. At her happiest, she lived with the fear of bad things lurking round corners, waiting to happen.

It was a fact of life, she thought. Everyone was allowed a certain amount of happiness. For some people it was spread out over seventy years or more; a thin layer of contentment that they experienced day after day. For others it was given in great blobs; a few years, months, weeks. Intense joy or pleasure balanced with periods of misery.

Her mum and dad had been happy, she was sure. One day they'd been chatting amiably over dinner, unaware that the next morning the postman would walk up their garden path and put a redundancy letter through their door. Kneeling down to pick it up, humming a tune from the radio, her mum might have simply put the letter in a pile, not realizing it would change everything.

Perhaps good times had to equal bad. There

was maybe some cosmic balance sheet that had to add up. A few years' bliss for a few years' pain.

Her fourteenth birthday had started as a glorious day. She'd woken up to find a leather jacket on the chair in her bedroom. It was on a hanger and still covered with plastic. It fitted perfectly, the exact style that she had pointed out to her mum on several shopping trips.

It made her look older and she wore it around the house before dashing out of the front door and along the road to Kate's house. Her friend had let out a squeal of delight when she saw the jacket, and then dragged Gina inside to show her what she was wearing for the party later that evening.

Gina had been allowed to invite six girls and six boys. The living room had been cleared of most of its furniture and they were going to use her parents' CD player. She and Kate had chosen the boys carefully, all kids that they liked and one or two that they fancied. Best of all was the fact that her mum and dad had agreed to go out for a couple of hours once the party got under way.

There were soft drinks and crisps. That was all. Gina had been adamant that she hadn't wanted sandwiches or cakes. The curtains had been drawn and only the tiny side lights left on so that the room was excitingly dark. Gina and Kate spent a long time getting ready, then they tried out some dancing, the music throbbing through the room. Gina jiggled up and down with delight at the way everything had turned out.

Then everyone arrived. The boys huddled up together in one corner of the room and the girls in another. There was an awkwardness that Gina couldn't put her finger on. Every time she tried to talk to one of the lads the others would snort with laughter and then lapse into play-fighting. When her mum and dad popped their heads into the room and said they were going to the pub round the corner, Gina thought that things might improve, people might relax; maybe it would be like a real party with everyone talking to each other and people dancing.

It got worse though.

One of the boys had a bottle of vodka and he took it out and offered to everyone. At first Gina had refused. It would upset her mum and dad, she knew. But when Kate held her paper cup of Coke out to let the boy pour some of the vodka in she decided to do the same. Alcohol, she knew, was part of being grown-up.

In a short while almost everyone had had a couple of drinks and one of the other boys pulled out two half-bottles of whisky. Gina tried some in her Coke and winced at the taste. She drank it anyway and found herself feeling light-headed. Looking round the room she noticed that the groups were no longer standing apart from each other but mingling. The music seemed louder and Kate had started to dance along with a couple of other girls who were all smiling and laughing. Gina heard herself laughing at nothing in particular and found herself looking at a lad in her class who she liked a lot. He came across and tipped the bottle of whisky so that she could drink some more. Then he put his arm loosely round her shoulder.

Across the room she could see a couple of the girls kissing some of the boys. In a very short while the party had taken off. She even felt like dancing but when she took a couple of steps across the floor she felt unsteady and had to stand very still in order to gain her balance.

Kate was dancing wildly in the middle of the room, her arms in the air, her legs kicking out. She seemed to be turning round and round and some of the boys were watching her and shouting things out. The music seemed to fill up every bit of space in the room and Gina couldn't hear anything that was being said. She looked round for the boy who'd given her the whisky. She couldn't see him for a moment and then saw that he was sitting on the floorboards in a corner kissing one of her friends.

Her shoulders drooped with disappointment and she finished her Coke and put the paper cup on to the mantelpiece, leaning back unsteadily against the wall.

Sometime around then she began to feel sick and slid down until her bottom was on the floor. She should get up and go to the bathroom. It was the drink, she knew. Too much of it when she wasn't used to alcohol at all. She didn't want to be sick, not in front of everyone. If she could just put her head down on the floor, maybe the nausea would wear off and she would be all right. The wood of the floorboards was cool against her face and she could feel the beat of the music vibrating through them. She closed her eyes, just for a few seconds. If she could sleep for a few minutes she knew she'd be fine again.

The living-room light came on suddenly, stunning all of them. Her mum marched into the room and straight across to the CD player and turned it off.

"The whole house is vibrating!" she shouted. "We could hear the music as we turned the corner of the street."

Gina watched her mum from the floor. She saw the side of her shoes and her legs and heard the anger in her voice. It had all gone wrong. She should get up and say sorry, but she couldn't.

Then she was sick. It came from deep in her stomach like something forcing itself up her throat. Her mum was looking at her in disgust. Everyone was staring in her direction. The floor was a mess and she could smell the vomit. Lifting her head up she saw her mum holding one of the whisky bottles. Her mouth was opening and closing and everyone was looking very unhappy. Gina didn't care. Her eyes forced themselves shut and she put her hands over her ears.

It had been a disaster and she had paid for it with weeks of unhappiness. That was the way of the world. She was more grown-up than that now, though. Being with Tony had made her like that. She had made love to him and that had made them closer than before. It was a secret that they shared; that knowledge of each other. No one else in the world had it. She felt a perpetual thrill playing about her shoulders. She looked at herself differently. Her mum and dad would just see Gina, their daughter, revising for her GCSEs. Kate would see her best friend, a boffin, a worrier. But Tony Campbell had seen her exposed; he'd seen her at her weakest and at her strongest. No one else knew her like that.

The thought of it made her want to turn the CD player up as high as it would go and dance around and sing out at the top of her voice. In quiet moments though, she knew it was too perfect. There were pitfalls. She could get pregnant. She could get caught. She could get dumped. She had to be ready. She had to look into the future and avoid all the possible traps.

It couldn't be spoilt, not this time. This was happiness that Gina was determined to cling on to.

15

The Careers Fair was in the main school hall. It had been cleared of the usual stacks of assembly chairs and set up to look like an exhibition. There were lots of borrowed screens and small islands of tables devoted to different career choices: Financial services (*Working in a bank*, Kate had said, dismissively); Caring services – nursing and social work; Engineering sciences – building, plumbing, electronics; Emergency services – the police and paramedics; Tourism and Catering (*Waiting tables in some hotel*, Kate had scoffed).

"What exactly do you want to do?" Gina said, exasperated at the negative comments.

"I've told you. Me and Jonesy are going to set up our own retail business. Lots of people do it. All the big stores started on market stalls. Even Marks and Spencer!"

There was never any point in arguing with Kate. She was so *certain* about everything. Gina was sure that her friend had never had a single doubt about any of the things that she had done or the plans she had made.

"This is all very well, but where's the stand for becoming a rock star or an international fashion model?"

Kate laughed at her own joke and shoved an open packet of strongly flavoured crisps at Gina.

"No thanks," Gina said. "You know you're not supposed to be eating anyway."

"Oh, stuff that. It's not like there's any teachers here."

That wasn't true. Gina could see the year head and two or three other senior teachers standing around talking to the exhibition organizers and the people from local industry. Kate was crinkling the crisp bag exaggeratedly.

"Your trouble is that you can only ever do what you're told to do. Honestly. If I eat a bag of crisps here, is it going to upset everything? Is it going to lessen the number of careers available? Are any of these nice, well-dressed industry types going to take a blind bit of notice? Look at that woman over there in the catering stand. I'll swear she's eating a McDonald's."

Gina didn't answer. There was no need, really. Kate was just speaking her thoughts aloud and Gina had heard them before. She looked over at the woman on the catering stand. She did seem to be munching on something.

"Loosen up, Gina. In a couple of months you'll be out of this place. How will you cope when there's no one around to tell you what to do. Whose permission will you ask then?"

Gina wasn't offended by Kate's strident tone. She smiled quietly to herself. There, just below the surface of her thoughts, were her memories of Saturday night. Kate's words had sent a ripple across them and a hazy picture emerged. Tony and her in the half-darkness lying across his bed; the clock on his bedside cabinet at 10:42 and beside it, catching the light on its corners, the crumpled cellophane of the condom packet. Something had been digging into her ribs, she remembered. She'd lifted herself up and pulled out her lemon satin bra that had become trapped. He had laughed, taken it off her and placed it gently on a nearby chair.

Kate knew nothing of this. If she had she might not have been so ready to mock her.

"What are you smirking at?" her friend said.

"Nothing."

Kate would be shocked. Not at the sex, but at the fact that it was she, Gina Rogers, who had taken the plunge without the usual weeks of soul-searching. At first she wouldn't believe it. *You went and bought some condoms?* She'd question her closely for every single detail. *Was it in a bed? Where were his parents?* Nothing would be sacred. *Were the lights on? Did you take all your clothes off? Did it hurt?*

"Are you seeing that Tony Campbell again?" Kate's voice burst into her thoughts. She was blowing air into the empty crisp bag.

"Probably," Gina said casually, as though it didn't really matter one way or another.

"Look. There's the place where you can open a bank account," Kate said. "They give you a free CD voucher and a pencil case if you sign up."

"But—"

Gina was about to remind her friend that she already had a couple of bank accounts when she noticed the young woman on the bank stall. It was Shelly Martin. She was standing behind a table talking to one of the teachers. She was wearing a smart blue suit with a cherry red scarf at her neck. She had a badge on that said *Shelly Martin, Accounts Advisor* and she was holding a wad of glossy leaflets. The teacher was brimming over with pride, introducing Shelly to some of the students as one of her old girls. Shelly was smiling widely and looked like she was basking in all the attention.

There was a young black man at the desk as well. He was wearing a suit and some rimless glasses and was working on a laptop computer tapping keys and talking to some of the boys from Gina's class.

Gina was about to turn away when Shelly noticed her and gave a little wave. She looked behind, thinking that it was for someone else, but it wasn't. She smiled back, feeling quite pleased with herself. They'd only come into contact with each other once and Shelly Martin was acknowledging her.

She left Kate queuing up and wandered back to the Emergency Services stand. There were loads of kids milling around, some looking at a video that had been set up in the corner. On it was a series of accident scenes with paramedics talking about their experiences. A couple of metres away was the Metropolitan Police display. Standing in front of a wall of posters was Sergeant Hamley, in conversation with a couple of kids from another class. He looked at her and gave a half-smile. Then he turned away to talk to a nearby teacher.

Her good mood dissolved. Sergeant Hamley seemed to have that effect on her. She looked down at her feet to see her black leather shoes. Her new trainers were at home in her wardrobe. A niggle of guilt made her shoulders twitch. Then, instead of thinking about the stolen trainers, she began to think about her mum on Saturday night, when Tony dropped her off. *Did you have a good time?* she'd asked, cheerfully not mentioning the fact that it was twenty past eleven. Her dad had been there too. There'd been some old-fashioned pop music on and the two of them had been laughing and joking. All the fury from the morning and the broken cup had disappeared. She'd stood watching them and felt her stomach fold up as though she'd been doing something terribly wrong; as though she'd betrayed them in some way.

"Hi, Gina."

A hand tapped her on the shoulder and she turned round. It was Eve Cole. Gina smiled.

"I wanted to thank you for the other night."

"What?" Gina said, puzzled.

"When you helped Marvin out."

Gina thought for a minute.

"Outside the precinct. That racist guy. He told me about it."

"Oh that," Gina said. "I didn't do anything. It was just this old white guy mouthing off. I didn't even think Marvin noticed particularly. He didn't seem put out by it."

"Oh, he was. I know Marvin comes across as being flash sometimes, but he's quite sensitive."

Gina didn't answer. *Sensitive* wasn't a word she would have used to describe Marvin.

"How is he these days? I've not seen him around school much lately. Is he keeping out of trouble?"

"He's been keeping a low profile," Eve said. "He's not hanging around with the same kids these days. There was some trouble up at the Track and the police brought him home. My mum was out so she never knew about it. He says he's turning over a new leaf."

"Do you think he will?"

"My mum's promised him a computer if he stays out of trouble till the end of the term."

"A computer?"

Gina thought about Marvin Cole messing round with the ball in the precinct. She also remembered him tearing around the playground in pursuit of someone or other. That was the thing about Marvin. He was never still.

"You'd be surprised. You should see him on a PC. He can do spreadsheets, desk-top publishing, the internet. He's really good at it!"

"That's going to cost her a bit," Gina said.

"Exactly. That's what I said. What kind of message is Marvin getting? Be a bad boy and then get the promise of a computer if you improve. Like, me? I've been good all my life and what do I get?"

"A blank cheque to spend down Oxford Street?" Gina said.

"I wish!" Eve said, wistfully.

"Never mind. Are you still hanging round with that kid who works in Tesco?"

"Nope. Dumped him. He never had any money. You still seeing Tony Campbell?"

"Sort of… Kind of…" Gina found herself stuttering

"Look at this!" Kate's voice squealed out, loud enough for several people to turn round. In her hand was a plastic see-through pencil case.

"What happened to the CD voucher?"

"I get that when I make my first deposit of twenty-five pounds!"

"Wow!" Eve said, rolling her eyes exaggeratedly.

"I can't wait!" Kate said, making a face.

"I'm off. Thanks again for looking out for Marvin," Eve said, and walked off to join her friends.

Later, after the Careers Fair was over, Kate and Gina waited around for Jonesy to come and pick them up in his car. They were sitting on a small wall at the side of the school. Kate had taken her tie off and was using it like a ribbon on her hair. Gina was sitting quietly thinking about Shelly Martin and Luke Thompson. Behind them, in the staff car park, the industry people were loading up their stands and displays.

Why had Shelly given Luke up? He was good-looking and had money. They'd been going out for a while, Tony had said, so she must have liked him once. Maybe there had just been something missing. Maybe it was like her and

Martin Wilson. He hadn't been bad-looking, but his keenness for her had put her off.

"I saw the Thompson brothers out in their jeep the other day," Kate said, as if reading her mind. She was looping her tie around one ankle and then trying to pull it off the ground.

"Um…"

Gina turned around to the staff car park just as Shelly Martin emerged from the building holding a couple of plastic boxes. Behind her was the young black man who had been on the stall as well. He must have said something funny because Shelly was laughing.

"Jonesy says they make most of their money by buying knocked-off gear."

"Their dad's rich," Gina said, turning back. She had the desire to add, *that's what Tony says*, but fought it. She didn't want to turn into another Kate. The sound of a nearby car door slamming made her turn round. Shelly Martin was sitting in the passenger seat of a red Peugeot. The young black man was opening the driver's door. He got into the car and put the key in the ignition.

The beep of a car horn sounded from down the road.

"Here's Jonesy at last!" Kate said, using her tie to wave frantically at his car.

Gina stood up and stretched her legs. She

glanced round at the car park behind. In the red Peugeot Shelly Martin and the young black man were kissing.

She was taken aback. It wasn't a long passionate kiss. Just two or three quick pecks on the lips.

"What are you looking at?" Kate said.

"Nothing."

Shelly had a new boyfriend. Gina wondered if Luke knew. She picked up the pile of leaflets she'd collected from the careers stalls and followed Kate in the direction of Jonesy's car.

16

It was a family conference. Gina's mum was sitting at the corner of the kitchen table. Her dad was opposite. Gina was between them.

"We need to have a talk. All three of us," her mum said, in a businesslike voice.

Gina was immediately worried. It must have showed on her face because her dad smiled and reached out his hand to her.

"It's nothing to worry about, love."

We're going to get a divorce were the words she expected to hear. *We're going to separate and you have to choose who you want to live with.*

"We know things haven't been wonderful lately," her mum said.

She was sitting upright at the table, her fingers resting lightly on the wooden surface. Gina noticed that her nails hadn't been painted and a couple were broken. Looking up, she saw that her hair was flatter than usual and she had no lipstick on.

Her eyes strayed to an envelope in the middle of the table. It was lying upright and had her dad's name and address typed on it. Someone had written, in neat print, the words FIRST CLASS and underlined them.

"Your dad and me, we've decided to give it one more go."

"What do you mean?"

One more go. The words were probably said to make her feel better, but they had the opposite effect. To her they sounded like *one last chance*. Her parents only had one last chance at their marriage. After that they would fail.

"Your dad's not been able to get a new job and it's put a strain on us all."

Her mum wasn't looking at her. She was focusing on the table surface. Her words were dull as though she was repeating a speech she'd been forced to learn off by heart.

"I've been offered a job, you see," her dad said, as if by way of explanation.

The letter sat in the middle of the table like a small boat in a big sea.

"In that big new DIY store down on the industrial estate. It's the biggest in Europe, they say!"

"That's great," Gina said, her voice low and croaky.

"It could be a new start," her mum said, "for all of us. Once the money starts coming in it'll take the pressure off."

"Things'll get back to the way they were before. Back to normal."

Her mum looked up for a moment and Gina caught her eye. There was no happiness in her look, no joy at all. A smile appeared on her lips but it was paper-thin.

"So I'm taking mum away this weekend for a break."

"It's not really a whole weekend," her mum said, "just overnight Saturday. We're going to Cirencester."

"We're going to spend some good old-fashioned time together," her dad said, reaching across and taking her mum's hand.

"You could stay over with Kate, couldn't you?" her mum said, her hand lying limply in her dad's palm.

"Yes, course."

She smiled at both of them. Inside though she felt this bubble of sadness. The job had come too late. Their marriage couldn't be fixed. She knew it and her mum knew it. It was just her dad who was in the dark.

Tony had bought her a present. It was wrapped in silver paper and he waited until they were alone in his kitchen to give it to her.

"What's it for?" she said.

She took it with trembling fingers. Her face

was still red, she was sure, from where she had been crying. Tony had been sympathetic, had pulled out a lump of kitchen roll for her to dry her eyes on. *Perhaps you've got it wrong*, he'd said. *Maybe this weekend is the very thing that will bring them back together*.

She doubted it. After the discussion, her dad had continued washing up the dinner dishes and singing along to a pop song on the radio. Her mum had gone upstairs to have a shower. She'd followed her up there and found the bathroom door locked, but no sound of the shower running. Instead there was a lot of sniffing and she called, *Mum are you all right?* to which there had been no answer. After a few seconds, the door opened and her mum emerged, her face red, a bunch of pink tissues in her hand like a screwed-up flower.

"Aren't you going to open it?" Tony said, excitedly.

She pulled back the silver paper with great care. Inside was an opaque bag with the name of a local department store. Placing the silver paper on the table she opened the bag. She took out some pale cream underwear. A pair of pants and a brassiere.

"Do you like them?" Tony whispered.

"Yes," she said, not looking up.

The underwear was made of fine lace, more

delicate and pretty than anything she had ever owned. She smoothed it down with her fingers but still did not look up at him, afraid that her face had reddened again, this time from embarrassment.

"What's the matter?" he said.

"Nothing. It's great. They're lovely."

Just small lace shapes that sat on the table between them. It seemed wrong. They should be hidden away under skirts and blouses, to be searched for and touched and ultimately discarded; not looked at in broad daylight amid the cups and saucers and the ornamental cat teapots.

"They're really lovely," she said, finally looking up at him.

"You can wear them for me. Next time."

The next time they Made Love. She smiled foolishly and brushed the fluff off her blouse. He caught her hand though and held it firmly, forcing her to look directly at him.

"Don't be embarrassed by it. It's natural."

"Is it?" she said.

He leaned over and kissed her lightly on the mouth. From behind she heard the sound of footsteps and the kitchen door opened. She snatched up the underwear and put it in the bag as Mr Campbell came into the room. Mrs Campbell followed a couple of steps behind.

"Sorry. Have we interrupted something?" he said, smiling benignly. He was holding a newspaper.

"Nope. I'm just going to run Gina home."

Tony's parents sat themselves down at the table. His mum's hair had been pulled back into a small bun and there were corkscrew curls at each cheekbone. She had a pair of tinted glasses on that Gina hadn't seen before. Her top was a brilliant midnight blue and there were pearl buttons down the front. Mr Campbell's cheeks looked pink, as though he'd just stepped out of a bath, and he was wearing an open-necked shirt with a small crocodile on the breast pocket.

"Shirley's just going to help me pick tomorrow's winner," he said, producing a pencil from behind his ear. Mrs Campbell was opening the newspaper out on to the table.

They were always together; in the kitchen, making tea, or on their way out shopping. She thought of her own mum and dad, always separate; he in the kitchen or garden, she watching TV by herself or upstairs sorting out her clothes or reading.

"Let Gina pick a number," Mrs Campbell said.

"Good idea! Go on Gina. Any number between one and twenty."

She looked at the two of them, their stout

bodies overlapping on the table. They were so happy in each other's company.

"Two," she said.

"Two. Oh yes. That's a good one. Ten to one. His colours are purple and green and he performed well last season."

"Come on, Gina," Tony said, rolling his eyes and guiding her by the elbow out of the door.

They drove part of the way in silence. Gina was clutching the present Tony had given her, wondering if she could get into the house without anyone noticing what she was carrying. She looked at her watch. It was ten thirty. In normal circumstances her mum would be doing one thing and her dad another. Since they were trying for a reconciliation though, they might be together, sitting side by side on the settee, discussing their plans for the weekend.

"Did you say your mum wants you to stay at Kate's on Saturday?"

"Yes."

"Why don't you ask her if you can stay at my house instead?"

"I'm not sure..."

"You could sleep in my room and I'll be on the sofa bed in the living room. I won't have to rush to take you home so early."

"My mum would never allow it."

Kate's mum would have allowed it. She would have said yes without a qualm. Kate wouldn't even have to make an argument.

"I'll get my mum to ring her up. One mum to another. She'll reassure her."

"She'll never let me."

"Trust me. My mum is very persuasive."

They drove round the corner of her street. Tony was moving about excitedly in his seat. He had plans; they could go out to the Spider's, get a takeaway meal, watch the late-night film.

Gina didn't bother to curb his enthusiasm. Let him find out for himself. Her mum would never allow it.

17

The lace underwear was lying on the bed. It looked fragile and light, as if a slight puff of air would blow it away. It made all her other clothes look heavy and cumbersome. Gina picked it up and held it up to her face.

A tiny knock startled her. She quickly tucked the underwear under her night-dress as the door opened.

"Mrs Campbell came into the branch today. She asked me if you could stay over at your boyfriend's house on Saturday."

Gina's mum was leaning on her bedroom door. She was still in her uniform, her badge – *Harts Building Society: Ms Donna Rogers* – was still on her lapel.

"What?" she said, guiltily smoothing the duvet down, only half-hearing what her mum had said.

"Your boyfriend's mum insists I call her *Shirley*, and said you could stay over there on Saturday night. She assures me she'll keep an eye on you both. You'll sleep in his bedroom and he'll sleep on the sofa bed."

"Oh," Gina said, embarrassed.

"I was surprised that you hadn't mentioned it."

"I thought you'd say no," Gina said, truthfully.

Her mum gazed around Gina's bedroom. She looked distracted, as though she was thinking of something else. Gina was puzzled. Was she saying she could stay round Tony's house? Or not?

"I laughed actually. I said to her, my Gina's a sensible girl. There's no way she'd do anything silly."

Gina frowned. She couldn't tell whether her mum was being ironic or not. The disastrous birthday party had been over two years before and had been largely forgotten. Every now and then though, whenever she asked for something important like permission to stay out late or go somewhere out of the area, the memory of that party would resurrect itself and sit silently between them like a sulky ghost. It was never mentioned, but there were always long silences in her mum's answers as if she was recalling the whole evening before deciding whether Gina was allowed some new privilege.

"I told Mrs Campbell that you could stay."

"Oh," Gina said, surprised.

"Actually, I trust him more than I trust that

silly Kate. You'd probably end up doing all sorts if you stayed there."

Gina made a face. In the aftermath of the party her mum had decided to blame Kate for a lot of what happened. Kate had probably brought the drinks, she'd said, or at least organized for them to be there. When Gina had protested she had simply tutted and said some things about Kate being *too headstrong for her own good*. It had been months before her friend felt comfortable in her house again.

"I don't really like you staying anywhere," her mum said, and left a long silence while she looked vacantly up at the ceiling of the room. "But since I've agreed to this weekend away, I've got no choice."

Gina sighed. Her mum emphasized the word *weekend* as though it was some sort of terrible chore.

"So, I can stay?" Gina said, pulling her back to the subject.

"Yes. Make sure you make up your bed and offer to help Mrs Campbell with the washing up. Perhaps you ought to take a bunch of flowers as well. I don't know why I'm saying this to you. You know what to do."

Her mum gave a little smile and pulled the door closed behind her.

Gina felt her shoulders relax immediately.

She lay back on her bed, her hands behind her head. These days she simply didn't feel comfortable in a one to one conversation with her mum. She was always afraid that her mum was going to *confide* in her about her marriage problems; as if her dad was some strange man who neither of them had strong feelings for.

On top of that, she knew that she wasn't being honest with her mum. She wasn't lying exactly, but she wasn't telling the whole story. She pulled out the bra and pants set from underneath her and let her fingers feel the crinkly texture of the lace. She would be sleeping in Tony's room and he would be on the sofa downstairs, but it wasn't the whole truth. That too had to be hidden in one of the long silences that happened between her and her mum these days…

The noise of the doorbell ringing came from downstairs.

Did she feel guilty?

No, strangely enough she did not. After the drunken party she had walked around for weeks feeling burdened down with blame. Every time she looked at her mum there seemed to be an expression of hurt on her face. She couldn't exactly put her finger on it. Sometimes her eyebrows were puckered up or her mouth was in a wrinkled line or her eyes were staring heavily around the room. Whatever the expression was,

Gina felt it was directed at her and a heavy dragging feeling would materialize in her stomach.

This time it was different though. Sex was a natural thing. She had chosen a decent boy who cared about her and she was taking precautions. What was wrong with that?

She heard her mum's voice calling. "Gina, there's someone to see you."

Had Tony come to find out what her mum had said? She took the bra and pants and put them underneath her other underwear in a drawer. Then she took a quick look in the mirror and skipped down the stairs expecting to see him. When she got into the living room her mum was talking to someone else.

"You've got a visitor," her mum said, smiling.

It wasn't Tony who had come to see her. It was Shelly Martin.

Gina carried two mugs of tea into the living room.

"I hope you don't mind me coming to your house," Shelly Martin said, as Gina placed the tea on the table.

"No, of course not."

Gina didn't mind at all. She was curious though. She and Shelly were barely on nodding terms.

The older girl was wearing a brown jacket and

matching trousers and looked like she had just come from work. Her long hair had been pulled back in a loose plait. Down at her feet sat a small case that looked like it held a laptop computer. On top of it rested a bunch of keys attached to a giant "S".

"I'm always losing my keys," Shelly Martin said.

Gina nodded.

"Are you still seeing Tony?" Shelly said, looking earnestly at her.

"Yes."

"I wanted to ask you a favour. It might be too late, I don't know…"

"Yes?"

"Did you tell Tony… Did you mention to Tony that you'd seen me with Trev?"

Gina looked puzzled for a moment.

"Trevor Walker. The man you saw me with in the school car park?"

"No."

She meant the tall black man with the rimless glasses. Gina remembered them kissing in the car. She hadn't said anything to Tony because she'd forgotten about it. All the stuff about her parents had got in the way.

"I know I don't have any right to ask you this. I mean it's not like we're friends or anything but…"

135

Shelly gesticulated with her hands as Gina looked expectantly at her.

"The thing is that I don't really want Luke to know that I'm seeing someone."

"I thought you and he were finished?"

"We are, but it didn't end very well. Luke was very upset and I know that he hopes we'll get back together again."

"You don't think you will?"

"Absolutely not. Luke's not actually a very nice person. He has a violent streak."

"He hit you?" Gina said, taken aback. She pictured Luke in his smart clothes, leaning casually on the jeep his dad had bought for him.

"No, not me. He'd never do that."

Shelly fished up the keyring and began to run her finger along the "S".

"No, he can be very nasty to other people. I've seen him in a fight. He's just wild. You wouldn't think it was the same person."

"And you think he might go for this bloke Trevor," Gina said.

"Very definitely. And not just because I'm seeing him. Luke and his family, they're ... I don't know quite how to describe it... They don't like black people."

"Oh."

"I mean ... they don't belong to any organization or anything and they don't go out of their way to be racist. Look, it was a couple of months before I even realized what they were like. That's when I knew I wanted out. I just had to let Luke down slowly."

"Tony's never said—"

"Tony's not really one of their close mates. I've never heard him say anything like that. I like Tony. He's a good bloke."

"Does Trevor know what Luke's like?"

"Yes. I've worked with Trev for about a year now. He's such a good person. He's funny and sharp. I'd just hate it if anything happened to him.

"Luke will find out some time."

"But not right now. Not while he's upset. That's why I'm asking you not to say anything to Tony. Like I said, I know we're not friends or anything. It's just that it'll avoid any trouble. That's all."

Gina sat for a minute, not quite knowing what to say. There was no real reason she should tell Tony. It hadn't come up in conversation and it probably wouldn't if she didn't bring it up.

"I won't say anything."

Shelly Martin heaved a sigh and seemed to relax. Gina actually felt like laughing. The whole thing seemed overly dramatic. Perhaps Shelly was exaggerating. Tony had said that Luke was upset, but would he really beat someone up because of it? She thought of him in his expensive clothes. Would he risk damaging his designer jacket or trousers?

"Tony likes you, Luke told me. He said you were just what he needed after Michelle."

Gina brightened up.

"What was she like?"

"I never knew her too well. Like I said, Tony's not one of Luke's close mates. I saw her a couple of times. She was really pretty, you know, and clever with it. She's going to university in September, I heard."

"Was that why it finished?"

Shelly Martin shrugged her shoulders.

"All I know is that Tony wanted someone different. He said he was fed up with someone disagreeing with him all the time. Maybe he just wanted a quiet life!"

Shelly Martin started to jingle her bunch of keys around. She suddenly noticed the mug of tea that sat untouched on the table.

"Oh, sorry," she said.

"That's all right. It's probably cold now."

"I really appreciate you not telling Tony about … you know…"

Shelly picked up the case at her feet and stood up to go.

"It's not a problem."

Gina was telling the truth. It was a detail that

had no importance whatsoever and she was happy to keep it to herself. Let Luke Thompson find out for himself, in his own time.

She let Shelly out the front door and went back upstairs.

18

On Saturday morning Gina got up early to see her mum and dad off. The radio was playing loudly in the kitchen and her dad was packing some rolls that he had made up. Gina could hear her mum coming down the stairs, her footsteps slow and heavy.

"When do you start the job?"

"A week on Monday. The money's not much, but it's a job and there's a possibility of promotion."

"Have you got a good chance of getting that?"

"I don't see why not. I've been in car sales for years so I've got good experience of dealing with people."

The kitchen door opened.

"Are we almost ready?" her mum said.

"Yep! Just packing these."

Her dad pulled out a length of cling film and covered the rolls.

"What are you doing?" her mum said, a look of incredulity on her face.

"I've made some rolls. No point in paying those high prices at the motorway service stations."

"We're supposed to be on a holiday. You'll be suggesting bringing a tent next."

"Oh now, don't exaggerate."

Her dad laughed lightly, and her mum rolled her eyes in an exasperated way.

Gina smiled at each of them weakly. The jovial atmosphere was thin and ready to splinter. Her mum turned wearily and let the kitchen door close behind her. Her dad continued what he was doing.

"She'll cheer up. She's always like this at the beginning of a holiday. You know that."

Gina did. Her mum didn't cope well with travel of any sort. Her frosty silences and thunderous looks were legend. This time though, it was different. There didn't seem to be any dangerous temper lurking, it was as though she was tired before she had even started; she hadn't even got the energy to bite anybody's head off.

By the time they were ready to leave, her mum had cheered up a bit.

"Don't take any notice of us arguing, love. Will you be all right on your own?"

"Course I will."

"Don't forget to lock the house up before you go off to Mrs Campbell's this evening."

"I won't."

She gave her mum a kiss and waved as the car pulled away and turned out of the street. As it disappeared she felt a sense of relief. A part of her had been sure that they would have a row and cancel the whole weekend.

She was about to go back indoors when she saw a police car come round the corner. It was cruising along slowly, as though looking for something. She stood and watched it for a minute. Then she noticed Sergeant Hamley was in the front seat. She sighed heavily in consternation. Every time she turned round lately, he seemed to be there. The officer hadn't even spoken to her but it gave her an uneasy feeling just the same. The car crept along the road until it was level with her. The policeman leaned out of the window.

"'I'm looking for Mickey Campbell. Have you seen him?"

"No," she said, "why are you asking me?"

As soon as the words came out she regretted them. Why hadn't she just said *no*. She was on the defensive and it made her look as though she had a guilty conscience.

"I thought you were a friend of his."

"No. Not really. I just know him."

That was another stupid thing to say. She was going out with his brother. Of course he was a friend.

Sergeant Hamley had his hand on his chin and looked as though he was thinking hard. The other officer was fiddling with the radio controls. Gina wanted to go back indoors, but she was worried the policeman would construe it as some guilty sign.

Then she saw the stupidity of the situation. What was wrong with her? Why should she feel any guilt? She hadn't done anything to be ashamed of. She was about to turn and walk away when the policeman spoke.

"Nice trainers," he said, looking down at her feet.

She couldn't answer. She looked down and saw the white trainers bright and big, just calling out to be noticed.

"Thanks," she said eventually, coughing lightly.

She stood as calmly as she could while the police car crawled off up the street. As soon as it turned the corner she let out a long, silent sigh. Then she turned and went back in the house.

19

They had a meal and a drink at a pizza restaurant and afterwards Gina went with Tony back to his house. They found Mr and Mrs Campbell in the living room with Mickey. All three of them had glasses in their hands. The room was warm and brightly lit and there was a jovial atmosphere

"Hello, Gina," Mr Campbell said, as she walked in with her overnight bag.

Mickey Campbell waved a hand, regally. He was sitting on a giant reclining chair, his feet up in front of him as though waiting for a dentist. Mr and Mrs Campbell were side by side on the settee, Mr Campbell with his arm loosely around his wife's shoulder.

On the coffee table was an ice bucket and a small bottle of gin. Beside it was a giant bottle of tonic and a plate covered with slices of lemon. A bowl of crisps and another of mixed nuts and raisins sat further along.

"Want a drink, dear?" Mrs Campbell said, putting her own glass down.

"No, thanks," Gina said.

"I'm just going to take Gina upstairs," Tony said, "we'll probably listen to some music."

"All right, love. We'll be going off to bed in an hour or so. I'll make up the sofa bed before we go. Don't stay up too late."

"We won't."

Upstairs, Gina put her bag on to the bed. Tony put his arm round her and gave her a tight squeeze.

"I'll be back in a minute," he said. "I just want to tell Mickey that Hamley is looking for him."

As he left the room the phone rang downstairs. She heard his footsteps quicken and then he must have answered the call.

She started to unpack. She had a clean nightdress as well as jeans and a top to wear the next day. She had a small bag of toiletries and a magazine to read (not that she imagined she'd need it). At the bottom of her bag she had the lacy underwear. She decided to leave it where it was for the moment.

She sat down on the edge of his bed feeling awkward. The bedside clock said 22:47. She looked at the bed where she was going to sleep and felt her flesh prickle as though she was cold and had goosebumps.

He wasn't going to sleep with her, she knew that. He definitely had to sleep downstairs on the sofa bed. *His mum and dad wouldn't stand for it*, he'd said. Then he'd laughed and said, *I'll just have to wait until they're asleep!*

She had an idea what he meant. There was a picture in her head of him creeping up the stairs in the pitch dark, tiptoeing across the landing and into his own bedroom where she would be, wide awake and waiting for him. They wouldn't have to worry about anyone hearing them. *My mum and dad's bedroom's at the far end of the house and anyway, they sleep like the dead when they've had a few drinks.* He had talked about it with such confidence; as though he'd done it a dozen times before. She wondered if it had been with Michelle, but she didn't ask.

She heard a door banging from below and then his footsteps heavy and rapid on the stairs. When he came into the room he looked flustered.

"I've got to go out," he said, throwing open the wardrobe door and delving into a space at the bottom.

"Why? What's the matter?"

He pulled out a pair of jeans and a sweatshirt and threw them on the bed. He took his jacket off and placed it hurriedly on the bedside chair and kicked his shoes off haphazardly.

"I've got to get changed," he said, turning away from her to undo his trousers. She stood up and fiddled with her bag. She tried to avoid looking at him changing but the room was too small and she could only bow her head and pretend that she wasn't noticing. He slipped his trousers off and laid them across the bed. Sitting down, hardly noticing her presence, he pulled his jeans on.

"What's happened?"

"There's some problem. Paul Thompson wants me and Mickey to meet him."

He stood up and zipped his jeans and then pulled the sweatshirt over his head.

"Shall I come with you?" she said, not really understanding.

"No. No."

He said it abruptly. Then he looked at her worried face and stopped what he was doing.

"I'm sorry, Gina. It's just that Paul says Luke's in a bit of a state, so me and Mickey are going to see if he's all right. I'll be an hour, tops."

"Where?"

"The Track. But I'll be in and out. An hour, no more. You have a coffee. Go to bed. When I get back I'll come up and see you."

He knelt down by his wardrobe and pulled out a pair of white trainers. They were similar to the ones that he had given to her. Then he sat down on the bed and patted the space beside where he was. She sat down beside him and he kissed her quickly on the mouth.

"I'll be back in no time," he said, pulling the laces out of the trainer so that he could get his foot in.

"Did Paul say what Luke was upset about?" she said, thinking suddenly of Shelly Martin and her new boyfriend Trevor.

"It's probably something and nothing. Sometimes Luke just wants attention. Like I said, I'll be back before you know it."

He stood up, retrieved his wallet from his trouser pocket and pulled out a couple of notes. Watching him, she realized that it was the first ever time she'd seen him in jeans and trainers. He suddenly looked three or four years younger. Pushing the money into his back pocket he flung the wallet on to the chest of drawers, bent down and kissed her on the forehead.

Then he was gone.

She took as long as she could getting ready for bed. She tiptoed into the bathroom and had a quick shower. Then she brushed her teeth and took her make-up off. She put cream on her skin and sprayed herself with perfume.

She went past the top of the stairs on her way back to the bedroom. The living-room door was wide open and she could hear the canned laughter coming from the TV. She closed the bedroom door behind her and wondered what she should do. It was too early to go to sleep, but she didn't want to go downstairs and sit with his parents. She played around with the clock radio until she found a station she liked. With the music playing low she reached into her bag and got her magazine out.

She began to worry soon after that. Turning the pages of the magazine without really reading them, she began to think about Shelly Martin and her new boyfriend Trevor. She hadn't said anything to Tony, but perhaps Luke Thompson had found out from some other source. Was he looking for trouble?

She gave a forced laugh. Tony had gone up to the Track. She couldn't see Shelly taking Trevor to spend his Saturday night there. Perhaps Luke was simply upset and needed his friends around him.

Was that what boys did when they were upset? She hadn't thought so.

From downstairs she could hear the sound of doors closing and the old couple padding up the stairs. She put her bag on the floor and slipped her feet under the duvet, her magazine in her hand. A light knock sounded and Mrs Campbell spoke.

"We're going to bed now Gina, dear. We've left the bolt off the front door so that the boys can get in. See you in the morning."

"Good night," she answered, hoping they wouldn't open the door and peek in.

Their footsteps continued along the hall and she relaxed. The bedside clock said 23:53. It wouldn't be long until he was back. She got out of bed and went over to the mirror. Her face looked OK, her hair clean and full. Looking down she frowned at her nightdress. It was newish and she'd ironed it that morning. It had a flower pattern and looked like something a ten-year-old would wear.

She turned back to her bag and got the lacy underwear out. It only took her a couple of minutes to pull the nightdress over her head and slip on the bra and pants. Then she went back and looked in the mirror. The brassiere had wire underneath the cups and they pushed her breasts up high. The pants were made of see-through lace and had a small rosette on the front sitting close to her belly button.

It was a transformation. The underwear added three or four years to her age. Tony Campbell had done that for her. He had made her grow up. She looked at herself in the mirror and felt a heavy ache for him, her skin tingling as though he was there running his fingers across her chest, along her stomach.

Was this love? She closed her eyes and pictured him kneeling in front of her on that first day, fitting her foot gently into a shoe. He'd said he was *Prince Charming*.

Now she was in his house, in his room and waiting to get into his bed. The thought sent a shiver through her and she got back into bed still wearing the underwear.

She lay there feeling exhilarated. She was, she thought, very happy.

After a while she fell asleep.

20

When Gina woke the bedside light was still on. She rubbed her eyelids and sat up, even though she felt weighted down with tiredness. The bedside clock said 02:14. There were voices outside the door of the room, hushed words spoken in a rapid-fire way.

After a minute, the door opened and Tony came in. He was walking slowly, taking each step with care. As he came closer she saw that he looked flushed and his sweatshirt was dirty, as though he'd been lying on the ground. There was also a strong smell of alcohol.

"What—"

She started to speak, but he put one finger over his lips. Then he sat down unsteadily on the bed and leaned over, pulling at his shoelaces and not managing to get them undone. He lifted one foot up and pulled at it, discarding the trainer when it came off. When he did the same with the other one he seemed to lose his balance and swore softly under his breath.

"Are you all right?" she said, dismayed at the state he was in.

"It got a bit out of hand," he said, making himself sit upright.

His eyes were blinking at her and she realized that he had registered her sitting in the underwear that he had bought for her.

"I've had too much to drink," he said, his words slurred.

Then he lay down, the top of his body across the duvet and his legs hanging on to the ground. The trainers were lying at angles where he had thrown them off.

"What happened?" she whispered.

"It just got out of hand," he murmured, rubbing the side of his head on the duvet cover.

"Did you see Luke Thompson?" she said.

"A bit of trouble. Luke had whisky with him. Too much."

His voice was muffled though, each word seeming to be an effort. Then he lifted his hand up and shielded his eyes from the bedside light. She made a move to turn the lamp in the other direction when she heard a series of stuttering sobs. She turned back and saw that he'd buried his face into the bed and his shoulders were shaking.

"What's the matter?" she said, alarmed.

She put her arm around him. He felt hot and sweaty, as if he'd been running around. He didn't speak, but his sobs grew quieter until eventually he stopped.

"There was a fight," he said. "When we got there, Luke was having a barney with some kids."

"Why?"

He shrugged and pushed his face further into the bed.

"I never done any of it. I was just watching."

"You're not hurt?" she said, looking at his grubby sweatshirt and jeans, both smeared with mud and grass stains.

"No."

"Was anyone else hurt?"

"I don't know," he said, his voice croaking. "Yes. No. I wasn't involved. I was on the outside. I'd had a lot to drink. I didn't wait around."

"But you're back home. That's the main thing."

Gina pulled him close to her. He had been scared.

"It's all right," she said stroking his hair. After a while he seemed to grow calmer and she realized that he was dozing.

Disappointment enveloped her. All her expectations for the evening had come to nothing because two groups of young men had fallen out with each other in a muddy field.

Gina lay her head back on the pillow and remembered the fight at McDonald's. It had been at lunchtime on a warm, sunny day; an unlikely time for a fight. It hadn't started with a flare of tempers, an insult, an accidental look or push. It had been pre-planned. The boys from her school had got there early and had a territorial advantage. They'd taken their sweat-shirts and ties off and put them out of harm's way. While waiting they'd pretended to be fighting with each other. The boy with the purple teardrop under his eye had certainly been ready for it. He had got hold of a heavy bike chain in advance and had planned to use it as a weapon.

He hadn't been seen in school since. There was a rumour that he had been threatened. Kate said that he was scared stiff and that the police had told him to stay at home. Gina didn't know if this was true or not.

The fight that had started as a bit of lunch-time excitement had turned out to be brutal and bloody and Gina still felt a stab of nausea when she thought of the bike chain ripping across the blond boy's face. She closed her eyes and turned her head from side to side as if trying to shake away the image.

She heard Tony mumbling and looked round, remembering where she was. He was lifting his legs off the ground and on to the bed. He was making himself more comfortable. She felt a moment of distaste and tried to move him away.

After looking forward to this night all week she suddenly wanted to be alone. He moved closer to her, his weight on the bedclothes heavy and solid; she felt pinned down, unable to move.

"Tony," she said in a loud whisper, "Tony, you have to go downstairs to sleep. TONY!"

He lifted his head with a start and then pulled himself up into a sitting position.

"It was just a bad fight," he said, rubbing his eyes with his fist, "I was just there. It wasn't my fault."

He looked like a small boy explaining things to his mum. She felt a rush of sympathy for him. He'd got into a silly fight. That was all.

"Go downstairs and sleep it off," she said, softly. "I'll see you in the morning. You'll feel better then."

After a few moments he pulled himself up into a standing position and gave her a wave. Then he tottered off, closing the bedroom door behind him. She listened for his footsteps and then heard the downstairs door opening and shutting. No doubt he had just lain down in his clothes. At least he had taken his trainers off.

She clicked the bedside light off so that the room was in darkness. She tried to imagine him downstairs, sleeping off the trauma of the fight. Someone had been hurt. At least it hadn't been him. He had cried; he simply wasn't the fighting type; it didn't come in his stride; he probably hadn't even thrown a punch.

She felt easier at this and lay very still for a long time, her eyes wide open, staring into the darkness of the strange room.

21

Opening her eyes, she heard unusual sounds coming from outside in the street. A dog was barking along the way; car doors were slamming; the engine of a milk float was gliding along, its bottles clinking every time it stopped. There was also noise from downstairs. A radio was playing and she could hear voices from below, where the kitchen was. She could smell the aroma of cooking, of bacon in particular.

She pushed the duvet back, feeling hungry.

It was 8:06. She doubted that Tony would be awake yet. She imagined him slumped across the sofa bed, still fully dressed. She wondered if Mickey had been drunk. If so, who had driven home?

She crept along to the bathroom and brushed her teeth. She put her jeans and shirt on, covering up the lacy underwear.

How long would it be before she could wake Tony up? Would he have a hangover? Would he still be in a state about the fight?

She tidied up the bed and then packed her night stuff away in her bag. Some of Tony's clothes were still draped over the chair from where he'd taken them off in a hurry the previous night. She folded his trousers on the crease and hung them over an empty hanger. She picked his jacket up and before fitting it round the hanger she realized that his pockets were full. She took out his stuff and placed it by the wallet that he'd left the previous evening; the mobile phone, his credit card holder, a bunch of keys, some packets of chewing gum. He'd left them all behind. All he'd had was some money.

Why hadn't he taken anything with him?

She fitted the clothes into the wardrobe. When the doors were open she could smell the scent of aftershave; a sweet, heavy smell that made her stop for a minute. How long would it be before he woke up and came upstairs to see her?

His trainers were lying upside down on the floor, making the room look messy. She bent down to tidy them up. They were filthy, the ridges underneath filled with dried mud. She turned them over, intending to tuck them under the bed so that they'd be out of the way.

One of the trainers had blood on it.

She put her hand inside it and held it up. In a different light it looked like brown mud. Then she took it over to the window and looked hard.

There was a tidemark of dirt all round the shoe and it was mottled with clumps of mud. The bloodstain was different. It nearly covered the toe of the shoe and was smooth, almost like paint. Looking hard at the rest of the shoe she could see tiny specks covering the whole surface, dozens of them, halfway between brown and red, as though something had splashed up on to it.

Her mouth filled with saliva and she swallowed it back. It was definitely blood on the shoe. She picked up the other trainer and put both of them under the bed.

Tony had said that he hadn't taken part in the fight. He'd just been watching. How could his shoe end up splattered with blood?

She stood up and opened the bedroom door. Going out on the landing she saw that the living-room door downstairs was open. Did that mean he was awake? Was he up out of bed, so early? She walked lightly down the stairs and looked in at the sofa bed. It was empty, the bedclothes on it hardly ruffled. A voice from behind made her turn round.

"Hello, dear. You're up early. Look at this Ronnie, both these lovebirds up early. They can't wait to see each other."

Mrs Campbell was still in her quilted dressing gown and she had a net over her hair that covered a number of pink plastic rollers. A silver coloured clip held a kiss curl on each cheekbone. Mr Campbell had a green towelling dressing gown on that stopped at his knees. Underneath, his bare legs and feet poked out, looking pink and cold.

"Look at the state of me. I'd better go up and comb my hair out before I frighten anyone," Mrs Campbell said, in a silly, girlish way.

Tony was sitting at the kitchen table. He looked half-asleep still and his skin was the colour of wax. He gave her a half-smile, but his eyes never met hers.

"Would you like some breakfast, Gina?" Mr Campbell said.

"I'll just have a coffee in a minute, if that's all right."

"There's some in the pot. I'd better go up and get myself dressed. I'll leave you two to chat."

He gave Gina a suggestive wink as he left the room. As soon as they were alone she spoke.

"Are you all right? You look terrible."

"Not too wonderful," Tony answered, the words thick and slow.

"What happened last night?" she carried on, even though he didn't look like he wanted to talk.

"A bit of trouble. That's all. It all got out of hand. Some of it I don't even remember very well."

He leaned forward over the table resting his forehead on his hands. He looked like he was going to be sick.

"Were you involved in the actual fight?" she said, quietly.

"No. I told you. I was on the outside."

He lifted his head and looked straight at her. His eyes had dark circles under them. He was lying.

"How come your trainer's got blood on it?"

"What?" he said, looking puzzled.

"There's blood on your shoe."

She had hardly dared to say the words, fearful of what his reaction would be. There was a nasty explanation growing in her head that she didn't want to face up to. He sat for a minute, his eyes staring into space. He looked as though he was thinking hard, straining to remember.

"There's blood on it?" he said, in disbelief.

He stood up slowly, steadying himself on the table and walked past her without a word. She followed him out into the hall and up the stairs. He went swiftly ahead, but she took each stair individually, not wanting to get to the top. From another part of the house she could hear his mum and dad talking to each other, laughing at some joke or story.

In the bedroom, she closed the door behind her. He was kneeling in front of his wardrobe looking for the trainers.

"They're under the bed," she said.

He turned round and pulled them out. When he saw the blood he seemed to stiffen. He knocked the other trainer out of the way and slumped forward. He stayed like that, cradling the stained shoe, looking shocked.

She leaned against the wall. He had been part of it. That's why he had cried the previous night. It was the memory of what he had done, not what he had seen.

He still denied it.

"I wasn't part of the actual fight. It was Luke and Paul. It was their fight. Luke was upset about Shelly. He said these kids needed a good kicking."

Gina flinched at the words *a good kicking*. It was a phrase, something people said when they meant that someone needed some sort of punishment. She might have even used it herself. She hadn't ever meant it literally.

"I was sort of involved. This kid, in the fight, he had a nosebleed. I went over and helped him up. His blood must have dripped on my shoes. That's it. That's what happened."

Tony pulled himself up off the floor, still holding the trainer. He sat on the bed, nodding his head as though he had just worked something out.

"That's what happened. That's where the blood came from."

He wasn't telling the truth, she was sure. He looked awful, dishevelled in his dirty jeans and sweatshirt. She'd never seen him look so scruffy before. She'd never even seen him in jeans.

His mobile phone started to ring. The sound was insistent in the quiet room and Tony looked momentarily annoyed. He leaned over and picked it up from the chest of drawers and spoke into it.

She looked at all the things that were on the wooden top. His wallet, his credit-card holder, packets of chewing gum, his mobile phone.

He was speaking in monosyllables: *Yes … yes … no… Wait … no… Just keep calm…* and then he turned away from her, his voice disappearing into a whisper.

And then she realized. He'd deliberately worn his old jeans because he hadn't wanted to get his good clothes damaged. He'd taken none of his valuable things with him either, because he knew that he was going to get into a fight. Maybe it was worse; he'd gone up to the Track *looking for a fight*.

"No problem," he said, his voice louder.

He flipped the phone shut and turned back to look at her.

"I've got to go out," he said. "I'll give you a lift home. I just need to shower and get changed."

She didn't speak, she couldn't answer.

"It was just a fight," he said, as he passed her. "These things happen all the time."

He kissed her lightly on the side of the head and started to gather his stuff together for a shower.

In the car, on the way home, he explained it again.

"The kid's nose was bleeding. I bent down to see if I could help. That's how the blood got there. I'm not saying I didn't throw a punch or push or shove, but that's it."

When she didn't answer he continued speaking.

"Fights are a fact of life. It's what blokes do. Don't get yourself twisted up about it."

She looked at him. He had showered and changed and looked like the old Tony; the one she had been so taken with. Since the phone call he had seemed calmer as well, more in charge of what he was doing, more organized.

Maybe she was overreacting. All kids get into fights. Maybe he had been an onlooker, the way she and Gina had been that day outside McDonald's. If they had been boys they might have been drawn into the argument, lent a hand, got involved. It could be that it was as simple as that.

"I'll give you a ring," Tony said and leaned across to kiss her cheek.

As she went into her house she was struck by the silence and emptiness. There was no sound of the radio or TV, no smells of toast or cooking from the kitchen, no movement anywhere.

Making as little noise as she could, she went upstairs to unpack her stuff.

22

There was a ring on the doorbell about three. When Gina opened it Sergeant Hamley was standing there. He looked hot and bothered and was fanning himself with a pile of leaflets.

"Georgina Rogers?" he said.

"Yes?"

"We've met before, haven't we? You're one of the students from West Wood School?"

"Yes."

Gina looked up the street, behind the officer, to see if anyone else was there. There was no police car and no other dark-uniformed man or woman waiting on the pavement.

"Are your parents in?" he said, smiling pleasantly.

"No."

"Well, look Georgina. It's like this. I want to have a chat with you. I expect you'd prefer it if I did it when your parents were around…"

"Why do you want to talk to me?"

"Like I say, I could come back when your mum and dad are in."

"What's it about?" she said, more abruptly than she meant to.

"There was some trouble last night at the Track."

Gina felt her shoulders stiffen.

"What's it got to do with me?" she said.

"Shall I come in or go away and come back later?"

The street looked empty, not even a bunch of kids playing with a football. In the distance she could hear some horns sounding, as though there was a bad-tempered traffic jam somewhere.

"You'd better come in," she said.

She poured the policeman a mug of tea. He'd been pleasantly chatting to her, asking where her mum and dad were and how she was getting on in school. She'd answered in a polite way, as though he was just a kindly adult making enquiries. She'd taken a while to make the tea, using a teapot and letting it brew. She was fending off the time when she had to speak to him, her mind puzzling as to why he had come to see her. What did she have to do with anything? His words, *some trouble last night at the Track* kept replaying in her head.

"Somebody told me that you're quite friendly with the younger Campbell boy."

"Yes," she said, placing a china cup and saucer in front of him.

"Only there was an incident last night in which the two brothers may have been involved."

"Oh?" she said, taking a mouthful of hot tea and swallowing it down too quickly.

"Mr and Mrs Campbell say that you spent the night round their house. Is that right?"

"Yes," she said, brushing imaginary crumbs from the front of her sweatshirt.

"You were there all night?"

"Yes."

"Was Tony Campbell there all night?"

She said nothing and looked hard at the table. The policeman had already been to see the Campbells; he had already asked them if their son was there all night. Why was he asking her?

She coughed, covering her mouth with the side of her fist.

"Yes, he was," she said.

The policeman's eyes were boring into her and she found herself unable to look up and meet them. She heard him take a deep breath and she sensed that he seemed to be getting bigger, taking up the whole of one side of the kitchen table. Glancing up, she saw that his uniform seemed darker, the buttons done up more tightly.

"You know for a fact that he was there all night long? He didn't go out for a while?" Sergeant Hamley said, tersely.

"As far as I know. I went to bed about twelve. Tony slept on the sofa-bed in the living room. I didn't see him till this morning."

The lie came out easily and she attempted a smile.

"Right," the policeman said, "so, as far as you're concerned, he was there all night."

"Yes. As far as I know."

It wasn't the truth and it left the question still unanswered. She picked up her cup and drank as much of the tea as she could. Then she stood up and made a pretence of washing it up under the tap. She could feel him sitting quietly behind her. What he was thinking she didn't know and didn't want to know.

"You know what interests me?" he said, quietly.

She turned round to face him.

"You haven't asked me what the trouble up the Track was. I told you something happened, but you haven't asked what."

"I just assumed that there was—"

"Most people," he cut across her, his voice harder, "most people would be inquisitive, nosy even. They would want to know what the details were. It would be my job to tell them as little as possible, but they'd still ask questions. It happens all the time. But you? You didn't ask me anything."

"I thought you probably meant there was a … fight." She stuttered the words out.

Sergeant Hamley drank his tea down in silence and then stood up.

"You didn't ask, because you know what happened up there. Because your boyfriend was one of the gang that beat up the lad."

"What lad?" she said, her voice breaking slightly.

"The lad, the kid who was separated from his mates; the black kid. The one who's in hospital now on a ventilator."

"A black kid?" she said.

Shelly Martin's face came into her head. She remembered her sitting in the Peugeot car with the young black man by her side.

"But you wouldn't know anything like that, would you Georgina, because you were asleep and your boyfriend was asleep on the sofa downstairs."

The policeman turned to go and Gina followed him out of the kitchen into the hall, a thumping sound in her head.

"To tell you the truth," he said, pausing at the front door, "I actually don't believe the story that's going round. A gang fight, a kid separated from his mates. It's all too easy. Here's what I think happened. I think the Thompson brothers went up the Track with the intention of getting hold of someone. The first bit of trouble, groups of boys fighting, that's a regular Saturday night occurrence up there. I think they waited till it was over and then they targeted someone. They hung around and followed him out until he was on his own. Maybe they scared his mates away. I don't know. But when they finally got him on his own –"

Gina's eyes had glassed over. Her throat felt as dry as sand. She couldn't have spoken if she'd wanted to.

"– they surrounded him, played around with him for a while, then they gave him a good kicking."

The pounding sound in her head was continuing. In the middle of it she heard something else. The phone was ringing. She glanced at it and then looked back to the policeman.

"The lad didn't move for a while, Georgina. Three or four hours to be exact. Not till someone found him."

The policeman opened the front door and stood still.

"I'll tell you something else –"

Gina looked round at the phone. She should pick it up. It could be her mum and dad. It could be Tony Campbell. She wouldn't find out unless she picked it up.

"– I don't think that lad will ever recover properly. Not that I'm a doctor, mind you. But I've seen people after they've had a beating, and that lad isn't looking too good."

The front door closed neatly behind him and

Gina stood rooted to the spot. The phone continued to ring, but she couldn't answer it. She couldn't move back or forward, and the drumming sound in her head was louder than anything.

It was coming from her heart. A heavy thudding that was vibrating against the wall of her chest. Using her fist she rubbed hard at her ribs and swallowed rapidly a few times. The ring of the phone bored into her and she backed away from it and slumped on to the stairs.

23

Kate and Jonesy were getting out of the car as Gina came out of her front door. Kate waved and looked like she was going to come over but Gina turned away and walked up the street towards the precinct. She wasn't able to get involved in small talk of any kind. She didn't even look back as she turned the corner.

She went straight to the off-licence in the hope of seeing Shelly Martin. She stood outside and looked through the glass window to see if Shelly was in the shop. There was just an older woman serving a couple of young lads.

She walked past the small group of shops to the alleyway at the back. There was a flight of wrought iron stairs that led up to the flats above. She went quickly up, wondering if Shelly would be in. Then she stopped abruptly. What was she going to say? Why was she going to see her at all? She wavered on the step, not knowing whether to go on or turn back home.

They gave him a good kicking. The words hung in front of her like a newspaper headline that she couldn't ignore. It hadn't been a fight at all. Tony had lied about that. It had been a gang of boys against one. The Thompson brothers and the Campbells. Somehow they had found out about Shelly's new boyfriend and had cornered him.

Shelly would think that she had told Luke Thompson about Trevor. Gina continued walking up the stairs. She had to explain. What had happened up at the Track was not her fault.

She walked to the door of the flat and rung the bell. After a few moments she heard footsteps. Then the door opened and Shelly Martin stood there in front of her. She was wearing shorts and a tight top and her face was pink, as if she'd been jumping about. In the background Gina could hear music.

"Hi," Shelly said, looking puzzled.

Could it be that she didn't know? Sergeant Hamley had seen the Campbells and her. He had told them what had happened. Had he not yet informed Shelly?

"You don't know, do you?" Gina said, feeling herself ready to dissolve into tears.

"What do you mean? What's the matter?" Shelly reached out and took hold of Gina's arm.

The police might not even link Trevor to Shelly Martin. Why should they? She was about to speak when a worse thought occurred to her. What if they hadn't actually identified him yet?

If his injuries were that bad they might not be able to work out who he was.

"Come in and sit down. What's the matter?" Shelly's face had a stricken look on it.

A picture came into Gina's head. The trainer with the blood on it. He hadn't been involved, he'd said, and yet his shoe was stained with blood. She saw him in her head, like a still from a film: silhouetted in the moonlight, in some dark lane that led off the Track, his foot lifted as though he was kicking a football; on the floor lay a crumpled lad with a broken face.

"It's not my fault," she blurted out and felt a single hot tear slide down her cheek.

"Who's there, Shelly?"

A voice came from deep in the flat.

"It's Gina Rogers, that girl I went to see," Shelly shouted behind, leading Gina gently into the hallway.

"Who?"

The voice came closer and Gina looked up to see a young black man. The same man she had seen in the Peugeot that night in the school playground.

"Trev, put the kettle on. This poor kid's upset about something," Shelly Martin said.

Gina wiped her face with the back of her hand and looked at Trevor standing behind Shelly in the hallway. She'd been wrong. Trevor hadn't been attacked.

"No," she said, "No, it's OK. I've made a mistake."

They were both frowning. Then Shelly spoke. "You've not told Luke Thompson about me and Trevor?"

"No, no. Take no notice of me. I've got to go," she said, turning round and walking purposefully to the door. It had been a stupid thing to do. She should have checked her facts.

"Gina, are you sure you're all right?"

Once outside she headed for the stairs, ignoring the voice from behind. She had made a fool of herself. What would they think of her? She went down the stairs quickly, her thoughts wrestling about inside her head.

Walking round the front of the shops she found herself suddenly confused. She wanted to get away from Shelly, but she didn't want to go home. Neither could she face Kate and Jonesy and she certainly didn't want to go and see Tony Campbell. She sat down on the low brick wall that edged the shopping precinct. A couple of metres away were a line of rosebushes that had erupted into pink and orange blooms. They swayed gently in the breeze and she reached out and touched one of them.

She'd been wrong. It hadn't been Trevor after all.

Sergeant Hamley's explanation had made her think that. He had said that the lads had gone up the Track looking for a fight. She had even thought it herself. Tony had worn jeans and left his valuable stuff behind; he and the others had gone looking for a particular person. A black lad. She remembered then that Tony had only gone because Paul Thompson had rung him up. *Luke's in a bit of a state*, Tony had said before he left to go up the Track. She had assumed that Luke had found out about Shelly and Trevor and had gone looking for revenge.

That had scared her. The idea that Tony could join a pack looking for some kind of revenge. He wasn't that kind of person, she was sure.

That wasn't what happened though. There had been a fight, that was true, he had told her himself. But it hadn't been pre-planned. They hadn't gone up there *hunting*. It had been just as Tony said. A fight that had got out of hand. The policeman had said that a black lad was lying in hospital, but it could have been anyone. It was upsetting, no one was denying that. Tony had cried about it. He had made a mistake. Everyone does at some time. It had affected him. That showed that he was not a bad person.

She felt suddenly weak and steadied herself on the wall. She had the strongest feelings for Tony Campbell. How could he be a bad person?

After a while she got up and headed for home.

About an hour later Kate came round.

"Have you heard the news about last night?" she said, walking past Gina through the hallway and into the kitchen.

"About the fight, you mean?" Gina said, following behind.

"The police have pulled the Thompson brothers in for questioning. I told you they were a bad lot."

Kate walked to the fridge and opened the door. She took a long look at what was inside. Gina pulled a chair out and sat down on it. Had the fight become common knowledge?

"Course, their dad'll get them some expensive solicitor and they'll be out in a couple of hours. Meanwhile Marvin's in hospital on a machine. They don't know if he's going to pull through. Even if he does, he might have brain damage. Eve's in a terrible state about it."

"Marvin?" Gina said.

"I told you those Thompson boys were trouble."

"What do you mean, Marvin? What's happened to him?"

Were they talking about the same thing?

"I thought you said you knew," Kate said,

pulling a half-empty bottle of Diet Coke out of the fridge and closing the door. "Marvin Cole got badly beaten up last night."

Gina didn't speak. This was information she didn't want.

"Want a drink?" Kate asked.

Gina shook her head. This couldn't be accurate. What did Marvin Cole have to do with the Thompson brothers? He was just a kid from school.

"Apparently he and his mate were cornered. His mate managed to make a run for it, but Marvin didn't. Knowing him he probably gave them a bit of lip or something."

Kate poured the drink out and then replaced the bottle in the fridge door.

"They gave him a terrible beating. One of the policeman told Marvin's mum that they left him for dead."

The word *dead* sounded hard and solid, each letter made from heavy stone. Gina stared at the wall behind Kate.

"Just as well your Tony was spending the night with you!" her friend said, with a half-smile.

"I don't understand. Why Marvin? He's only a kid."

"I know. The police think it might be a race thing. I told you about those Thompsons. They're

180

not nice people. Jonesy told me that the other week when you started seeing Tony Campbell. Their old man was put inside for beating up some black bloke who bumped into his wife and made her spill her drink. Bad-tempered or what?"

She didn't answer. There was this gaping hole opening up inside her. Her Tony hadn't been with her, he had been part of a group who were beating a schoolboy up in a dark lane. *They surrounded him*, the policeman had said, *they played around with him for a while. Then they had gave him a good kicking*. There was a sick feeling in her throat and she tensed to stop it from spilling out.

"Are you all right?" Kate said. "You don't look well."

"I'm not," she said, cupping her hand over her mouth.

Then they gave him a good kicking. She closed her eyes and saw Tony's trainers scattered on the bedroom floor. They were almost identical to the ones he'd given to her on that first day. He'd knelt down in front of her and said, *Prince Charming, me*. When she'd looked closely at one of the shoes she'd found a schoolboy's blood on the toe. He hadn't done anything, he'd said, but she knew that he had been part of the kicking. That's why the blood had been there.

She stood up, her hand over her mouth. She was going to be sick. She took a couple of steps over to the sink. Bending her head she retched dry and hard.

"Gina, what's the matter?"

But nothing came out and she continued staring at the base of the sink with her mouth open and her throat heaving.

As if it could all be cured that way; as if she could get rid of the terrible feeling that she had by letting it pour out of her mouth. Tony Campbell was just like the others. He'd put the boot in; maybe more than them. He was not a good person.

"Gina, what's wrong?" Kate had her hands on Gina's shoulders and gripped them tightly.

"Everything," Gina said, between sobs.

PART THREE
giving tony up

24

It was possible to stop loving someone. Gina wasn't a fool. She knew that. Her mum had stopped loving her dad some time before. There were little signs and Gina had noticed them, but they hadn't really *registered* with her.

Years before, when they had first moved on to the estate, they had been content. She had been eight years old and remembered the thrill of running into the empty rooms, her feet echoing on the wooden floor, as the removal men followed with the furniture.

It was a new house when they moved in, and although her mum had been grateful to move out of the flats, she had only lived in it a couple of days when she announced that it was like a cardboard box. It was in a way. Gina had looked round her own bedroom, its flat, biscuit-coloured walls, its sharp corners, its oblong window. She quite liked that idea and she and Kate had got hold of some shoeboxes and made them into little houses for their dolls.

Her mum bought her dad a workbench, a peculiarly ugly metal table that folded flat and could be hung on the wall. He had been delighted with it and spent hours putting it up and down, reading the instructions and looking at the variety of things that could be done with it. He bought himself some tools and made a special set of shelves in the garage to keep them in order.

Her mum had often found him there and Gina had watched from the garden as she stood, with her hands on her hips, pretending to be exasperated, asking her dad whether he was *ever* going to do any actual decorating.

They did each room up one by one. Gina remembered the smell of the paint – heavy, mildly medicinal – and the little rolls of wallpaper left over from a strip, like patterned sausages lying around the floor. She had collected them for a while and had an idea that if someone bought her a dolls' house she would do it up. She outgrew the notion though, preferring clothes and make-up as presents; grown-up things, just like Kate had.

Whenever anyone commented on how nice a room looked her dad always attributed the flair and style to her mum.

"It's nothing to do with me," he had said, when Kate's mum had asked about the brightly-coloured walls and bookshelves in the living room. "It's Donna who's the arty one. She designs it. I'm just the workhorse."

Her mum had stood brimming with pleasure, rubbing the back of her hand on her dad's arm, giving him secret looks and smiles that ended, some time later, in giggles and shrieks from behind their bedroom door.

It was a comfortable time. Gina could walk through the house at ease, with no worries about stumbling on one of their spiky rows or falling headlong into one of their bottomless silences.

There were visits to DIY centres, garden centres, furniture warehouses. There were pictures cut out of magazines and Sunday supplements, books of wallpaper patterns, paint colour charts. Best of all were the packs of curtain samples; little pads of material squares, all different. She and Kate had cut one up and made it into a quilt cover for their dolls.

Over the years, the house slowly changed. The contrasting colours altered its depth and the furniture and pot plants and shelving made square rooms look curved and mysterious.

Then her dad lost his job.

Was that when her mum stopped loving him? Or had it been in the years leading up to it when her mum got the job in the building society?

Every day, when Gina dragged herself into the bathroom to get ready for school, she found herself enveloped in the smell of her mother's deodorant, her perfume, her body spray; little floral clouds that lingered after she had gone out in her blue uniform with her badge that said, *Harts Building Society: Ms Donna Rogers*.

Her dad had welcomed the job at first. They'd be able to think about buying the house, he'd said; they even got lots of brochures and planned holidays abroad.

Had it just been on one day that it had changed? Had Gina left a house full of soft humming and singing in the morning only to come home to a crashing silence in the evening?

She couldn't remember. All she knew was that the love had gone. She saw it every day in her mum's eyes. Only her dad didn't know it yet.

On her bed was the lacy underwear. She'd washed it and dried it in the airing cupboard and laid it on the duvet. From downstairs she could hear the sound of the TV. Her mum was watching something. Her dad was out tidying up the car after their weekend away.

Just as she was about to put her nightie on she stopped and walked over to the mirror. Letting her towelling dressing gown drop off her shoulders she looked at herself. Her body was thin, her breasts tiny, her pubic hair pale and slight. Her skin was pink after her shower and felt dry to touch. She ran her hand across her stomach. She remembered the first time that

188

Tony Campbell had done that. Her breath caught for a minute in her throat. He had spent an age running his fingers all over her skin and she had lain back and felt her head drowning in pleasure.

She pulled her dressing gown roughly around her. Her throat was full up again and she tried swallowing back a few times.

Marvin Cole had been the centre of Tony Campbell's attention for a short while. His physical contact with Tony had been brief and brutal. There had been no kindness, no mercy.

Was it possible that one person could be so gentle and so hard at the same time? She picked up the underwear from the bed and held it tight. She had trusted him; without a thought she had opened herself up to him and he had turned out to be someone quite different from the person she had loved. Wait, that's not strictly accurate. She couldn't use that word *love* any more. It didn't fit anything now. She hadn't been in love because the person who had enthralled her hadn't really existed.

The young, well-dressed man who drove a car and gave her things and was smart and funny and gentle was only one side of the person. That night at the Track he was something different. A Jekyll and Hyde story.

She felt angry, and pulled at the bra and pants

as if to tear them apart. Then she opened her bedside drawer and picked out a small pair of silver nail scissors. She began to chop through the fabric, pulling bits of it and hacking through the rest with the tiny silver scissors. It took a while but she didn't mind; it was something concrete to do.

In the end, her dressing gown and the duvet were covered with tiny particles of cream fabric. She stood up and brushed them off and they seemed to swirl up momentarily, before fluttering sadly down until they rested on the carpet like spent confetti.

It was all over.

Gina understood that now.

25

On the way home from school, Gina heard the beep of a car horn. She turned and saw Tony Campbell pulling up by the pavement. Part of her wanted to walk on, but she knew she would have to see him eventually.

"I've been ringing you," he said, when she leaned down to the passenger window.

She nodded, her face stiff. She'd told her mum and dad to say she wasn't in; that she was in the shower or had gone to bed early. Her mum had asked her if they'd had a row and she'd said they had.

Further along the road she could see Kate. Her friend quickened her step towards her and Gina groaned. She'd told Kate most of it and she'd had a plateful of advice. She had no appetite for any more.

"Get in. We can have a cup of tea round my house. I'll take you home afterwards."

It was the last thing she wanted to do, but she got into the car anyway. During the journey he chatted lightly about his day at work, his super-visor, and a man who returned a stereo saying that it hadn't worked properly from the day he'd bought it. His voice had sounded a bit strained and he kept looking sideways at her before turning back to the road.

She ummed a couple of times but largely stayed quiet. She couldn't trust herself to say much to him.

His house was empty.

"My mum and dad are out shopping," he said, placing a couple of carrier bags on to the kitchen worktop. One of them held a biggish cardboard box that was covered with brown sticky-tape. Tony Campbell took it out and placed it to the side. Then he became businesslike and moved smartly round the kitchen, filling the kettle, getting the mugs out, putting the tea bags into them. All the time he was speaking under his breath. *Now where's the teabags, here they are, now the cups, there we go, is the kettle full enough, yes it is, press the switch, now we wait.*

He was still wearing his work clothes; the trousers of a suit and a shirt and tie. His sleeves were folded back so that the lower part of his arms were bare. He was as neat as a pin. She was still in her uniform, hot and sticky after a day in school. Her hair needed washing, but she hadn't wanted to do it. She had no make-up on, her skin was blotchy, her eyes puffy.

What had he ever seen in her?

A sense of sadness took hold of her. He had been perfect. An unexpected gift that had thrilled her to bits; a sudden win on the lottery; a birthday card with a fifty-pound note inside. The whole affair had taken her by surprise, grabbed her by the throat and dragged her into a new world. He had been her Prince Charming.

But there was something rotten about him and it had spoiled everything.

He poured the boiling water into the cups and gave her one. Then he lifted the cardboard box into the middle of the table and with a knife slit the sticky tape so that the box opened.

"I got this for Mum," he said, carefully taking out a china teapot and placing it on the table between them. It was a golden tabby cat in a reclining position. Its eyes had been coloured with some kind of glitter paint and they stood out, catching the light.

He saw her looking.

"What do you think? Do you think Mum will like it?"

"The police came round to see me," she suddenly said, ignoring his question.

"I know," he said, his face showing surprise at the abrupt change of subject. "You told them I was here all night. I'm really grateful."

He tried to look her straight in the face. He had the beginnings of a smile around his eyes and lips, but her stony expression seemed to stop him.

"I know you can't be happy about it. I wasn't completely honest with you. To tell you the truth I was in shock myself."

"What happened?"

She said it in a neutral tone. She wanted his side of the story. She wanted to see how he would describe it. He placed the cat teapot to one side and sat down opposite her at the table.

"Don't you go believing everything that policeman said. He makes it sound like we were a bunch of vigilantes or something. There was a fight, up the Track, like I told you. A few cars, a load of blokes, one thing led to another. There was a lot of booze. People always get more confident when they've had a drink. These black kids turned up. We weren't anywhere near them, but they stood out a mile. Everyone knows that the Track is a place where white kids hang out."

Gina frowned. She hadn't known that. She hadn't been there very often, it was true, but she hadn't realized that black kids didn't use it. She tried hard to visualize the time she had gone there with Tony. Had there been any black kids then? She couldn't remember.

"Don't misunderstand me. I've got nothing against blacks. They've got the places they hang round and so have we. That's all. Either way it didn't really matter. Someone would have told this Marvin to get lost. Trouble was Luke Thompson was upset about Shelly."

"He knew about her new bloke?"

"Did you know?"

Gina didn't answer. She didn't have to justify herself to him. Not any more.

"He saw her coming out of a pub with this black kid. Shelly was all over him, that's what Paul said. He was furious. Wanted to go and chin the geezer then and there, but Paul held him back. Funny really." Tony Campbell gave out a weak laugh. "If he'd hit the guy then none of this would have happened."

Gina's eye strayed to the golden-coloured cat. It seemed to be staring at her. He had bought it as a present for his mum; to please her; to make up for the fact that he had been a bad boy.

"Me and Mickey, we just went up there to keep Luke out of trouble. He'd been drinking and he was threatening to get in the jeep and drive over to Shelly's place. He was drunk, he could have hurt someone. We just wanted to calm him down."

He made it sound like he was a social worker doing a good turn.

"We played him along for a while, giving him more to drink. And I suppose it meant we were drinking more. I thought, if he gets drunk enough he'll fall asleep. He won't be able to get into a fight."

"But he did. You all did," Gina said flatly.

"The black kids didn't go home. They started playing round near us and Luke noticed them. It's like they were the only blacks there and Luke had this other black kid in his head. He started to get upset. He started looking at one of them, shouting at him. Then he walked over and shoved him."

Gina thought about Marvin outside the precinct when the old man had told him to go back to where he came from. She almost smiled, thinking of his cheeky answer. Tony Campbell must have noticed her expression because he relaxed suddenly and put his hand across the table on to her arm.

"That was all it was, see. If the kid had just gone home... But he started mouthing off back to Luke and then Paul got involved. The other black kid pulled at him and they started to walk away. But by then Luke wasn't having it. He was drunk, see, and confused, and he started having a go at this kid for seeing Shelly."

Tony Campbell's voice had lowered and he was looking pained.

"They started to run and Luke and Paul ran after them. Me and Mickey followed and I

196

swear, on my mother's life, I swear, that I was just chasing to stop them doing anything."

On his mother's life. How easily he used that phrase. Gina thought of Mrs Campbell with her sparkly tops and her lacquered hair.

"It went on for a while. They ran along these lanes that led round the back of the old stand. It was like hide-and-seek, you know, and there was a sort of excitement. I kept thinking, when we catch them I'll be able to stop Luke and Paul. We'll let them go."

He stopped speaking and she noticed that his hand was rubbing at her skin. She pulled her arm away and made herself look directly at him.

"You beat him up just because he was black, because he reminded Luke of Shelly's boyfriend?"

"No," Tony Campbell raised his voice. Then he lowered it. "Yes. No. It wasn't that planned. I've told you. We were chasing them and then one of them skimmed up this fence and got away. The other one just stood there. He wasn't scared, see. He just stood there giving some cheek."

"Why didn't you let him go?"

"He kept on and on, this kid, and then Luke went in and gave him a pasting. He fell down and pulled Luke on top of him and Luke was struggling. He was too drunk to do anything and this black kid was holding Luke close to his chest and Luke was choking, we could hear it.

Paul ran forward and kicked him. So did Mickey. It all happened so quick. I was going to stop them, but when I heard Luke screaming out I just..."

She could tell that he didn't want to finish the sentence.

"You kicked him too."

"I think so. I wasn't sure, you know, at the time. But when I saw the shoes."

"So four of you were kicking a fourteen-year-old kid while he was lying on the ground."

Tony Campbell stiffened.

"I'm not proud of it. I'm not pleased with myself. I didn't mean it to happen like that. It wasn't supposed to go that far. It wasn't."

From the hallway Gina could hear the sound of the front door opening. She heard the voices of Mr and Mrs Campbell.

"Do they know?" she said, standing up to go.

"Not exactly. They know I was there, but they don't know about the trainers..."

He meant that they didn't know that he had done any of the kicking. They thought, just as she had, that he'd been an unwilling onlooker at a nasty fight. Boys will be boys. He'd got into a bad crowd and had been pulled into something that wasn't his fault. Gina had seen the blood though, and now she knew different. She turned to go, just as the old couple came into the room.

"Hello Gina, dear," Mr Campbell said.

"Hello, love," said Mrs Campbell. "Oh, look!"

The cat teapot was sitting looking serene, its eyes glistening under the electric light.

"Did you buy this for me? Oh, you are sweet."

Mrs Campbell gave her son a hug and winked at Gina. Tony Campbell had a weak smile on his face.

"I must go," Gina said. "My mum's expecting me for tea."

She smiled at the three of them and turned to go. A couple of moments later she heard Tony following her.

"I'll drive you," he said, his car keys in his hand.

During the drive he told her about the Thompsons.

"They've been arrested. The other kid, he told the police that it was two brothers with a jeep. It didn't take the Law long to sort out who it was. They've got a solicitor though. There's no one to identify them. It was dark, everyone was drunk. There's no way they'll go down for it."

"What about your trainers?"

"I chucked them in the river."

She thought she saw a grin on his face. It could have been a grimace. She wasn't sure. After a few minutes they turned into her street.

"I just want to get this all over with. Then we

can all get back to normal," he said, pulling into a parking space near her house.

She should end it. She should have the courage to tell him she didn't want to see him again. Kate would have done it. She would have told him what she thought of him in a couple of piercing sentences. But it was an effort and she was tired of talking.

"Shall I ring you tomorrow?"

"If you like," she said, dully.

"OK. And Gina," he said, putting his hand on her shoulder and leaning across to whisper in her ear, "thanks for sticking up for me with the police. I won't forget it."

She watched him drive away with a heavy heart. He hadn't mentioned Marvin Cole at all. It didn't matter to him that the boy was in a bad state in the hospital. He was sick. He might have brain damage or, worse, might not wake up at all. All Tony Campbell cared about was excusing his own role in the fight. That and her having provided an alibi for him with the police.

Now he was going home to his mum and dad, all brimming with pleasure at the stupid cat teapot. A few streets away another family house was empty. Marvin's mum and his sisters were probably all up at the hospital wringing their hands and consoling each other about what had happened.

She sat on her garden wall and thought about Eve Cole. They had been close friends once. Whatever had happened to that? There had never been an argument or a fight that she could remember. One day it had been her, Kate and Eve hanging around together and then Eve had been sitting down the other end of the dining hall with a group of black girls.

It hadn't been sudden; it had probably happened over days, or weeks even. One lunchtime Eve had stopped to have a chat with some girls from her street, the next she had spent break with them. After that it had been walking home together and sitting in the same row in assembly. She and Kate hadn't minded at all.

Then one day she was gone. She wasn't their close friend any more, she was someone else's. Had it been a black and white thing? Perhaps Eve had felt more comfortable with girls who were black. Possibly she and Kate made Eve feel left out because they were white and she was black.

It was a question she couldn't answer. She didn't think so. For her and Kate race had never been an issue.

Would they have let a white friend go so easily? Wouldn't they have been hurt? Perhaps made recriminations? Been stroppy with her for dumping them? But there had been no hard feelings; they had watched her go with a shrug of the shoulders. What kind of friendship had that been?

She looked up and down the street. There were groups of kids playing football and a few hanging round on bikes. All of them were white. Then she thought about the houses. Her immediate neighbours were white, as well as those across the road. As her eye travelled further up and down the street she tried to think of houses where black or Asian people lived, but there were none as far as she knew.

Had growing up there made her into a different kind of person?

Eve's brother had been in hospital for nearly four days and she hadn't gone to see him. She hadn't even gone to see Eve. Was that because Eve was no longer one of her best friends? Because she was black? Or because it had been her boyfriend who put Marvin in hospital?

Perhaps, she thought bitterly, it was a mixture of them all.

26

Gina knew where the hospital was. She'd been there on a school visit once. A small group of them had been doing a project on nursing and they'd been given permission to go in and look around. She'd been with two other girls, all studious types, and they had followed a male nurse around and taken notes on the information he gave. Gina had seen the different wards: the children's, the surgical, the geriatric. She'd even had a tour past the operating theatres and seen the table and the rows of instruments, the giant lights and wired-up computers.

This time she was going straight to one place: Sunflower ward, on the third floor. She'd rung the hospital earlier and asked where Marvin Cole was. He was only seeing family, they'd said, but she wasn't intending to visit. In her hand she had a bunch of roses, pale yellow. There was a card attached and she'd written a message in it. *I was so sorry to hear about what happened to you. I hope you get well soon. Yours, Gina Rogers.*

She almost lost her nerve as soon as she stuck

down the envelope. Sending flowers to a badly injured boy wasn't going to do anyone any good. It might even make her look worse. There was every chance that Tony Campbell's name had been mentioned to Eve and her family by the police. Eve knew very well that Tony was Gina's boyfriend.

Still she decided to go. Not for Eve or her family, but for Marvin himself. Afterwards, whatever happened, she wanted him to know that she had been concerned.

She followed the signs up to the ward. The ward sister was behind a long desk and Gina crept up to it, intending to leave the flowers and go. The woman nodded distractedly when she explained and Gina decided not to linger. Turning back towards the exit she walked straight into Sergeant Hamley.

"Georgina Rogers," he said, surprised.

"Hello," she said, taking small steps round him to get nearer to the exit, "I was just bringing some flowers for Marvin."

"Right," he said, turning round so that he was still facing her.

"I must be off," she said.

"We had to let the Thompson boys go," he said, looking straight at her.

"Oh," she said, nonplussed.

She stood for a minute not knowing what to

do. She should go, that's what she'd planned. He opened his mouth to speak again though, and she couldn't be that rude. She didn't want to talk to him, not at all. But she couldn't just walk off.

"No evidence to hold them. The other lad, who was with Marvin, he couldn't pick either of them out of a line-up."

"That's a shame," she said.

"Marvin's in a bed, just round the corner. He's conscious now. Why not come round and see him?"

"I couldn't. It's only family who's allowed."

"There's no one with him at the moment, and anyway we can make an exception. Come on. It will cheer him up to see someone new."

He cupped her elbow and led her gently along. She hung back though. She didn't want to face him. Even though she hadn't been to blame she felt, by association, a responsibility for his being there.

"Georgina, just come and say hello. It'll make him feel he's getting better if people other than just his family come to see him."

On the other hand, perhaps it wasn't such a bad idea. Seeing Marvin awake might calm her, make her feel better. If she could see that he was on the mend then none of it would seem so bad.

She walked alongside the policeman through the ward to a door at the end.

"He's in a room by himself," Sergeant Hamley said.

He opened the door and she followed him in. Not wanting to look directly at the bed she focused on the vases of flowers that lined the window sill. There seemed to be hundreds of flowers, all in various stages of bloom. There were roses and irises, freesias and lilies. There were carnations, dozens of them, with chrysanthemums in pots at the edges. Some of the blooms were brazen and loud, some of them leaned tiredly over the side of the vase, their best days over.

"How are you Marvin? Look, I've brought someone to see you."

She had expected him to be awake, sitting up, the hospital table across his bed. He could have been playing solitaire or holding a Gameboy. He could have been watching the TV or reading a magazine. He wasn't doing any of these things.

He was lying flat on the bed and when Gina looked at his face she felt her stomach drop down to her feet.

"Hello Marvin," she said, her voice shaking.

He was flat on the bed and his scalp was wound up with metres of bandage. His face was visible but not something that she wanted to look at for long. One of his cheeks had ballooned up as though it had been filled with air. His eye had sunk in beneath it and his forehead had a long cut that had been stitched up, reminding her momentarily of a film of *Frankenstein* she had once seen.

His arm was in plaster and attached to a wire that ran along the ceiling to the bottom of the bed. There were dressings on his chest and at the base of his throat.

"How are you?" she said, thinking, as she said it, how stupid it sounded.

There was a half-smile from him and she could see that his eyes were bright and he knew who she was. He didn't speak though.

"He can't say anything at the moment," Sergeant Hamley said. "His larynx has been damaged."

"Oh," she said.

"Somebody stamped on it."

She had to hold on to the bottom of the bed. Her smile was still on her face but inside she felt as though she was cracking up into little bits. *Somebody had stamped on it*. She closed her eyes and swallowed hard. When she opened them she saw Marvin's weak smile and felt her heart like a fist in her chest.

"We won't stay, Marvin. I'll bring Georgina back another time."

Marvin seemed to move his head in a tight nod. Gina turned and followed Sergeant Hamley out of the door. When it closed behind them she felt her nose fill up and she knew she was going to cry.

"I must go," she said.

But the police officer had his hand on her arm and pulled her over to the side of the ward. Then he spoke very quietly in her ear.

"That's what your boyfriend and his friends did to Marvin. We know they did it, but we've got no witnesses, no one who'll come forward."

She leaned away from him, but he held her close.

"You're the only one who can help. If you break Tony Campbell's alibi then it won't be long before we have the rest as well. Think about it."

Then he let go of her and walked off up the ward. She watched his shoulders recede, square and disapproving; his steps determined and swift as though trying to put as much distance between them as possible. She felt herself adrift among the beds and the drip machines and the harassed nurses. She wanted to get out but had momentarily lost her sense of direction.

She saw Eve Cole and her mum walking through the ward. She stepped back into a corner half-hidden by a giant food trolley. She did not want to face them. She could not speak to them. They passed only a couple of metres away and for an agonizing second she thought that Eve's eyes met hers. There was no sign that she had registered her there and the pair went on into the tiny ward where Marvin was lying with his throat taped up and his head stitched back together.

For a long time she floated around the ward and the hospital corridor thinking and worrying.

Then she made her decision.

PART FOUR
after tony

27

If anyone had been betrayed it had been Gina.

She stood outside her front door with a rag dipped in white spirit and rubbed at the black paint. The word BITCH stared back at her as she wiped from one side to the other. When that did nothing she focused on each individual letter until some of the paint at the edges started to give. She could feel perspiration forming under her arms and her breath coming in short quick gasps. Stopping for a moment, she looked up the street and saw a group of small kids watching intently, their tricycles and bikes upended on the pavement. Their mothers were standing with them, their arms folded. These were women that she and her mum and dad spoke to regularly, but they didn't offer her any sympathetic smiles or tut or roll their eyes. They simply watched her, their faces set with disapproval.

It was just as Kate had said. *You don't grass people up. Let the police do their own dirty work.*

A police car turned the corner just at that moment and pulled up quietly by her door. She groaned to herself. Her dad or mum had probably rung them. Sergeant Hamley got out and came up to the front door.

"I'm sorry about this, Georgina," he said, rubbing his forehead with his hand.

"It was only a matter of time," Gina said, wearily. All her anger had gone. She was doing a job of work, cleaning the front door. Someone had been bound to find out. She had always known that.

"The Campbells worked it out. As soon as we charged Tony they must have known that you'd withdrawn your alibi."

Gina drew a heavy breath and continued to rub little circles into the door. Looking further into her own hallway she could hear her mum and dad's voices from the kitchen. It sounded as though they were having a heated discussion. Gina gritted her teeth; that was probably her fault as well.

"They don't know about the shoes yet. That evidence will come out at the hearing," the policeman continued.

On the day she'd gone to the police station, she'd taken Sergeant Hamley to the place by the river where she and Tony had parked on that first date. She had no idea whether Tony had thrown the shoes in there or somewhere else. The following day some police divers had retrieved a black plastic bag that held the bloody trainers.

"What about the Thompsons. Have they been arrested?" she said.

The policeman cleared his throat.

"Not yet," he said. "Tony Campbell isn't saying anything. When he sees all the evidence against him he'll talk. He's being brave now, but a couple of months on remand and he might not feel so charitable to the Thompson brothers."

Gina gave a half-smile.

"You're wrong," she said, bitterly, "he won't grass his mates up."

"You're not sorry that you came forward?"

"No," she said.

Was she sorry? The whole street was being frosty towards them. Kate hadn't phoned or come to see her since she had made her decision. Her mum and dad weren't speaking to each other. Her mum wasn't even speaking to her.

And yet there was Marvin Cole lying in a hospital bed, beaten up because he was black and had reminded Luke Thompson of someone else. The teenager who always had a cocky word for every situation now had no words at all. Marvin couldn't speak and so Gina had had to speak up on his behalf.

"How's Marvin?" she said, finally rubbing the

"B" off her front door, leaving what looked like a dirty mark.

"He sat up yesterday."

"And his voice?"

"Early days yet. There's a lot the doctors can do, but we'll have to see."

Gina noticed an old couple walking on the other side of the road, arm in arm, peering across to see why the police car was there. She also saw Kate and Jonesy's car pass by and felt an ache in her throat.

"It's early days," Sergeant Hamley said. "People will forget. In time, when the trial is on and the details come out, people will be on your side. You did the right thing. Sometimes, you have to take a chance and do the right thing."

She nodded and wondered if he was right. He turned and they went back to his car, the policeman giving her a wave as he got in. She felt disconcerted by his friendliness. She hoped it didn't mean that he was going to be seeking her out or chatting with her every time he saw her in the street. One brush with the police was enough.

She turned back towards her front door and saw, with surprise, Kate and Jonesy standing there, carrying bottles and sprays and packets of J-cloths.

"Here," Kate said, pushing a can of paint remover at her, "I always thought your front door could do with a makeover."

Jonesy gave a broad smile. In his hand he had some paint charts. Kate walked up to Gina and linked arms with her, pulling her back to her gate.

"I was a bit hard on you the other day. I hadn't thought it through, not really. Jonesy never liked those Campbells, not since school, did you?"

Jonesy shook his head pleasantly. Gina wondered if Jonesy had said it or whether Kate had put the thought into his head. Either way, it was nice to hear.

The three of them worked on the front door until almost lunchtime. By then, all the black paint had come off. Her mum had come out and sat on the front wall looking at the colours on the chart. After a while, her dad brought out mugs of tea and some biscuits. The atmosphere was brisk and there was a good deal of distance between her mum and dad. A few people walked past. A couple of them stopped and said something soothing, people Gina had seen, but never actually spoken to. The others just stared straight ahead as though they weren't there.

Eventually, when they finished, the three of them – Gina, Kate and Jonesy – went out to get something to eat. They walked along the street to the precinct. In the window of the news-agents there was a large advertisement for the local paper. The headline seemed to shout out at her:

POLICE MAKE ARREST
IN RACIST BEATING.

Gina looked around the tiny row of shops. There were about a dozen people milling about, among them three or four kids from her school. She fancied that they were all looking at her, that they knew she had been the one who had gone to the police. Kate saw her looking and slung her arm around her, while Jonesy went into the chip shop.

Gina looked from person to person, her eyes defiant, studying each face for some sort of reproach. She didn't care what they thought any more.

It had been the right thing to do.

Gina Rogers was sure of that.